P9-DHD-147

Sweet Masquerade

Sweet Masquerade

Marion Chesney

G.K. Hall & Co. • Chivers Press
Waterville, Maine USA Bath, England

This Large Print edition is published by G.K. Hall & Co., USA and by Chivers Press, England.

Published in 2001 in the U.S. by arrangement with Lowenstein Associates, Inc.

Published in 2001 in the U.K. by arrangement with the author.

U.S. Hardcover 0-7838-9612-3 (Core Series Edition)
U.K. Hardcover 0-7540-4728-8 (Chivers Large Print)
U.K. Softcover 0-7540-4729-6 (Camden Large Print)

The text of this Large Print edition is unabridged.
Other aspects of the book may vary from the original edition.

Set in 16 pt. Plantin by Christina S. Huff.

Printed in the United States on permanent paper.

British Library Cataloguing-in-Publication Data available

Library of Congress Cataloging-in-Publication Data

Chesney, Marion.
    Sweet masquerade / Marion Chesney.
      p. cm.
    ISBN 0-7838-9612-3 (lg. print : hc : alk. paper)
    1. Guardian and ward — Fiction.   2. England — Fiction.
    3. Large type books.   I. Title.
  PR6053.H4535 S94 2001
   823′.914—dc21   2001044356

For my friend,
Jenny Soo,
with love.

Chapter 1

The writing desk was placed in one of the bays of the library windows. Seated at the desk was Augustus, tenth earl of Berham.

Usually the window commanded a fine view of rolling parkland falling away to the dark line of the woods in the distance, but on this day it was raining. It seemed to have been raining for weeks, months, years: steady, drenching, depressing rain forming small lakes in the lawns, dampness in the great mansion of Berham Court, and discontent in the soul.

The earl carefully sanded a letter, folded it, dropped a blob of scarlet sealing wax on the fold, and stamped it with the heavy, crested ring he wore on the middle finger of his right hand.

Then he settled himself back in his chair and moodily watched the raindrops running down the window panes.

He was bored. As usual.

Boredom seemed to have been with him so long that he had trained himself to become accustomed to it, as his late father had become accustomed to painful rheumatism, and his late mother to awful and perpetual toothache.

He recognized the familiar, lethargic state for

what it was and tried to think himself out of it by reminding himself of the many things in his life which should have made him a grateful and contented man.

He was thirty-two years of age and in perfect health. He was accounted very handsome, but he cynically put down all female adoration as worship of his great fortune and rank. He owned the splendid edifice of Berham Court, a hunting box in Leicester, and a small draughty castle in Scotland. He had a townhouse in London which he visited to "do" the Season and, incidentally, disappoint the matchmaking heart of every hopeful mother in town.

Apart from the cares of his estates, he was tolerably free from responsibility. Or had been. For the earl was awaiting the arrival of his ward, Mr. Frederick Armstrong.

It had come as rather a shock to him when he had been informed that the late Colonel Armstrong, whom he remembered vaguely as a fiery and choleric eccentric, had willed his grandson to him, appointing the earl as guardian.

In vain had the earl's men of business searched for other relatives who might take the brat. The colonel had alienated them all so long ago that they wished to have nothing to do with his grandchild.

Frederick was reported to be eighteen years of age, a deuced difficult age to do anything with. He was too old to be packed off to school, and there seemed to be no evidence of any scholarly ability to suggest that he could be sent off conveniently to Oxford University without a great deal of cramming first.

The best thing, thought the earl, was to see the boy, and if Master Frederick proved to be healthy and sound in wind and limb, to buy him a set of colors and join him to a cavalry regiment.

His guardianship was to last until the boy reached twenty-one, when Frederick would inherit his grandfather's fortune.

Apart from his yearly visits to London, the earl was something of a recluse. In the country, he rarely entertained. The management of his estates and farms took up all his time. There were many female relatives who had tried from time to time to suggest that he needed the soft touch of a lady about the place, but he had parried their offers successfully, saying he was quite happy as he was.

And that, he realized with surprise, had been the case until a few months ago. He had not always been quite so bored. But once the harvest had been taken in and the countryside had settled down to its long winter's sleep, there had seemed little to absorb his mind or his interest.

His well-trained servants came and went like ghosts, anticipating his every need.

He watched the raindrops pattering against the glass, meeting and joining to form rivulets. The fire crackled behind him on the hearth, and the clocks ticked away the tedium of the hours.

He had sent his carriage to bring Master

Frederick home. Home? Well, he supposed Berham Court *would* be the lad's home until he decided what to do with him.

The blurred windowpanes threw back his reflection, a ghostly earl with thick black hair growing to a widow's peak on his forehead above a harsh and handsome face with a high-bridged nose and firm mouth. His eyes were coal black, the type of eyes which so rarely mirror the owner's feelings, Mediterranean eyes, a heritage of his Italian grandmother.

All at once he heard the faint rumbling of carriage wheels and the steady clip-clop of horses' hooves drawing nearer. Master Frederick was coming home.

There was a scuffle from the hall as the butler summoned the footmen to be ready to carry out the new inhabitant's bags.

The earl stayed seated, watching the rain and turning a quill pen in his strong fingers.

The carriage stopped outside, and the earl suddenly felt his boredom lift. It might not be so bad after all having a young man to teach and guide.

The double doors to the library were thrown open.

The butler, Hickey, announced, "Master Frederick Armstrong."

The earl got to his feet and turned around.

For a long moment Frederick Armstrong and the earl surveyed each other in silence, each fighting down feelings of disappointment.

The earl saw a small, slim boy in a dun brown coat, old-fashioned knee breeches, and buckled shoes. His hair was carroty red, and his eyes were very clear and very blue, with thick, curling lashes. But his face was pretty and girlish, and his small figure was so slight that it looked as if a puff of wind would blow it away.

Freddie Armstrong saw facing him a very tall and imposing man with broad shoulders, slim hips, and long, powerful legs. His black hair, growing to a point, combined with his coal-black eyes and handsome harsh face to give him a satanic appearance. The earl of Berham was not at all the kindly old gentleman Freddie had fondly pictured.

"You are not old," he blurted out, staring at the sculptured whiteness of the earl's cravat and wondering how such a miracle had been achieved.

"Did you expect me to be old?"

"I was led to believe that the Earl of Berham was . . . was . . . quite old," Freddie answered falteringly.

"I think that when your grandfather made his will, he was thinking of my father," said the earl gently. "They were great friends once upon a time."

"But I was left in the care of the *tenth* earl," said Freddie hopefully, as if already looking for a way out of the arrangement.

"I am the tenth earl. The ninth was my father. Come and sit by the fire and warm yourself. You have had a long and fatiguing journey."

Freddie punctiliously waited until the earl was seated on one side of the fireplace before cautiously seating himself on the other.

"Oh, the journey was *not* at all fatiguing, my lord," he said, his husky voice light and attractive.

"I had never been away from Hartley Manor — my home, you know — before. Grandpapa would not let me go beyond the boundaries of the estates. We never really saw anyone at all, either, and it was monstrous exciting to see all the towns and villages and people. . . ." Freddie's voice trailed away before the cold harshness of the earl's face. Impossible to know what the man was thinking, but Freddie felt as if he had been guilty of betraying ungentlemanly enthusiasm.

"In that case," said the earl, studying the boy thoughtfully, "we will discuss your future. Have you any ambitions to follow a military career?"

"No!" squeaked Freddie. Then, lowering his voice, he repeated, "No."

"In that case, what had you planned to do with your life?"

Freddie lowered his eyelashes. "I had not planned anything," he said in a low voice.

"Very well," said the earl. "I think we should begin by building you up a bit. You are very small and puny for your age. You are . . ."

"Eighteen, an it please your lordship."

"Young, but that is all to the good. Your

12

clothes are quite disgraceful. Are they all like that?"

Freddie nodded dumbly.

"I do not plan to go to town until the Season begins," said the earl, "but our local tailor can at least produce better than those shapeless garments you have on your back."

"If it please your lordship," ventured Freddie timidly, "I would like to keep my own clothes for . . . for the present. I have not yet got over the shock of Grandpapa's death, and he chose these clothes for me, and . . ."

"Oh, very well," said the earl testily. "I do not entertain much while I am in the country, but if we go to town, then you must dress as befits your station as my ward. If you are not fatigued, perhaps you would care to ride out with me this afternoon."

"I would like that very much," said Freddie. "I am not at all tired."

"Good. There is a prizefight in the neighborhood, and I promised to attend. Good heavens, lad! You look quite dismayed."

"Perhaps I am more fatigued than I thought," said Freddie, lowering those irritatingly girlish eyelashes.

"Well, I think you should make a push to come with me. Have you ever attended a prizefight?"

"No," said Freddie thankfully.

"Then you may count it as an addition to your education. Excuse me one moment. I have some things to attend to."

The earl rang the bell and ordered wine and biscuits to be brought. He stood up, and Freddie promptly jumped to his feet.

"You may stay here by the fire and have some refreshment until I return," said the earl. His black eyes raked over Freddie's slim figure, and he muttered something under his breath as he quit the room.

The butler entered, bearing a silver salver containing a decanter of wine and a plate of biscuits. He placed the repast on an occasional table, carried the table over to the fire, and set it at Freddie's elbow. A huge footman in green and silver livery came in with a basket of logs and piled several on the fire, and then both men bowed to Freddie and left him to his meditations.

Freddie sat and bit his thumb and looked nervously about the room. Ranks upon ranks of calf-bound books rose from floor to ceiling. Had the earl read them all? Probably, thought Freddie dismally. An apple wood fire crackled on the hearth under the marble fireplace, which depicted two Greek figures writhing in frozen ecstasy. Above the mantel, a grim-faced lady in the panniered dress of the last century stared down at the boy in haughty surprise.

There was a gilt French clock on the mantel, a grandfather clock in one corner, and various other clocks about the room, whispering and ticking, almost as if they were busily gossiping to each other and discussing this shabby interloper.

An oriental rug covered the center of the floor. In the middle of the room stood a console table, its marble top supported by a huge eagle of gilded pine, its spread wings appearing to hold up the top.

Freddie thought uneasily about the prizefight to come. Perhaps it would not be so bad. There would be people, lots and lots of people, and Freddie craved human company. All his life had been spent in the empty, dusty rooms of his home, Hartley Manor, with only his grandfather's harsh voice and eccentricities to supply any life to his lonely existence.

Perhaps a prizefight would not be so bad after all.

"Yesterday," says the *Protestant Mercury* for January 12, 1681, "a match of boxing was performed before his Grace the duke of Albemarle between the duke's footman and a butcher. The latter won the prize, as he hath done many before, being accounted, though but a little man, the best at that exercise in England."

And since that first record of a public boxing match in England, the sport had grown in popularity. Now, during this first decade of the nineteenth century, it had become more a religion than a sport, with worshipers of the art of pugilism traveling many miles to see their favorites.

And so, from a noble patron looking on at two men engaged in punching each other's heads, it

15

had grown to a science and an art.

Boxing was so popular that it became the fashion for a man of position to keep his own prizefighter, the duke of Hamilton and Lord Barrymore being two well-known patrons who enjoyed that luxury. The members of London society turned to taking lessons in the art themselves.

The chief of fashionable instructors was John "Gentleman" Jackson, at his famous rooms at 13 Bond Street, London. Everyone grew enthusiastic about Jackson, his manly beauty, his generosity, the astonishing fashion of his clients, "to attempt a list of which," said one newspaper, "would be to copy one-third of the peerage." Even the poet Lord Byron capered around on his lame foot and fondly believed he had the makings of a pugilist in him.

The prizefight to which Master Armstrong was taken, sitting up beside the earl in his sporting curricle, was held in a field outside the small country town of Berham.

The extreme fashion and popularity of the sport had drawn many Pinks of the Ton and Corinthians to the ringside. The ring was in fact formed more by the circle of carriages surrounding it than by the ropes held by posts.

The rain had slackened to a fine drizzle, and the grass around the ring was already churned up into a brown sea of mud by the hundreds of carriage wheels.

Freddie huddled miserably in a drab benjamin,

water dripping from his beaver hat onto his lap, and surveyed the scene.

There were, naturally, no women present. Most of the carriage audience were extraordinarily finely dressed considering the weather, and Freddie felt he was bringing shame to his guardian by being so shabbily clad.

The two contestants looked remarkably alike. Cully, the favorite, was small and stocky, with a massive chest and huge round head. Grigson, his opponent, was similarly built but was distinguished from Cully by his being completely bald.

The atmosphere was carefree and easy, and Freddie felt himself relax. There surely would not be much bloodshed and violence at such a friendly gathering.

The fight began. Utter silence fell upon the spectators as the combatants sparred for about a minute. Cully then put two most dexterous hits through his opponent's guard, in the mouth and on the throat at the same moment. Grigson fell like a log, covered with blood. Freddie studied his toe caps with great interest.

"What happened?" screamed a man behind Freddie.

"Cully hit him a blow on the victualing box," answered a swarthy man in the next carriage to the earl.

In round three, Grigson successfully planted a hit in Cully's breast and rallied, but Cully had the advantage of putting in most blows, although Grigson threw him. Grigson's head had begun to swell, and he bled freely. Odds two to one on Cully.

At the end of round six, Grigson put a tremendous blow on the side of Cully's head, and both fell out of the ring.

The earl glanced sideways at Freddie. The boy's face looked rather white, and his lips were moving as if in prayer.

By round seventeen it seemed to the stunned and bewildered Freddie as if he were attending a circus in ancient Rome rather than a fight in a field in nineteenth-century England. Grigson had twice turned his back on his opponent and made towards the ropes, but Cully followed him, changed his front, fibbed him, and kept him from falling until he had hit him into an almost senseless state.

By round twenty-seven Freddie was as white as paper. Grigson was brought down by a heavy blow under the ear, and then the twenty-eighth round decided the contest, Grigson being much too exhausted to be brought to the mark in time. The battle had lasted an hour and a quarter.

A mass of blood, Grigson lay on the churned grass, with the gentle rain mixing with his blood and running in little streams across his prone body.

With a choking, muffled sound, Freddie slowly keeled over and hit the mud under the carriage in a dead faint.

"What ails the lad?" cried several voices.

"Travel fatigue," said his lordship tersely as he swung himself down and gathered Freddie's inert body in his arms. "I should have made the boy rest."

He loosened Freddie's limp apology for a cravat and then doubled him over so that his head was between his knees. Freddie coughed and choked and was violently ill.

He blushed miserably and scrubbed at his mouth with his handkerchief.

"I think the physician, Mr. Campbell, had better give you an examination," said the earl. "Are you well enough to climb up?"

"Yes, please, sir," whispered Freddie. "I am very well now, thank you. And, please, my lord, I do not need the services of a physician."

"Your fainting spell shows weakness," commented the earl harshly as he picked up the reins. "You are still very much a child. I trust it was not the sight of blood which made you dizzy."

"No," lied Freddie, thinking that he would never forget the sight of that poor man covered in his own blood, lying in the rain. "Will he live?" he added.

"Grigson? Oh, yes." The earl condescended to unbend a little as he expertly drove through the press of carriages towards the road.

"I confess I do not find prizefights very amusing. Particularly the type of one we have just seen. Look! The sun at last."

A pale washed-out disc was floating high above hazy veils of ragged cloud. Somehow it made the February day seem bleaker than before. Water dripped steadily from the bare branches of the trees beside the road, and there was mud everywhere.

A muddy goose flew out from under their wheels, its wings outspread. A muddy peasant touched his forelock and gave a toothless grin, and a muddy sheepdog plodded slowly homeward along the muddy ditch.

Freddie shivered, feeling ill and lost in an alien world.

When they reached home, he was conducted upstairs by a stout housekeeper rustling with black bombazine.

He was led along corridors and left in his bedroom to put himself to bed. "My lord's instructions."

The room was dominated by a four-poster bed with blue and white hangings. The walls rioted with hand-painted Chinese wallpaper, a whole oriental forest of birds and leaves and branches. In the bay of the window stood two Chinese Chippendale chairs and a Chinese lacquered writing desk.

A small dressing room led off the bedroom in which Freddie found his shabby clothes looking lost and forlorn in an enormous mahogany wardrobe. There was a toilet table with two brass-bound cans of hot water, fluffy towels, and two cakes of Joppa snap.

Freddie found his nightshirt in a chest of drawers, along with his red Kilmarnock nightcap, and pulled them out. Making sure the doors to the bedroom and dressing room were locked, he stripped and washed himself down. Still shivering from the shock of the prizefight, he struggled into his nightshirt, crammed the red cap on his red curls and dived between the sheets, turned his face into the pillow, and wept with fear and loneliness.

A half hour later the earl tried the door of Freddie's bedchamber and found it locked. He testily asked the groom of the chambers to fetch the spare key and waited impatiently until it was brought to him. Suppose the boy were really ill!

At last the door was opened, and the earl marched in. Freddie was lying fast asleep, his tear-stained face cradled on one hand.

The earl felt himself becoming angry and irritable. The lad was little more than a babe. What on earth was he to do with such a milksop? It was too much responsibility. Here was no dream son to take shooting and hunting but a useless delicate lad who fainted at the sight of blood — for the earl had not believed Freddie's lie for a moment.

But he gave a little sigh and told the groom of the chambers, Mr. Dawkins, to awake Master Armstrong in time to dress for dinner. Then the earl made his way thoughtfully downstairs, where his butler informed him that Lady Rennenord had called with Mrs. Bellisle and that he had put both ladies in the yellow saloon.

The earl felt a slight stirring of interest. Mrs.

Bellisle was a wealthy lady who lived on the other side of Berham. It was in doubt whether there had ever been a Mr. Bellisle.

Lady Rennenord, a distant relative, recently widowed, had arrived a bare month ago to live with Mrs. Bellisle. She was a few years younger than the earl and already was famous for the beauty of her looks and the fashion of her dress. The earl had not met her, although he had seen her at a distance.

He retired upstairs to his bedroom and changed rapidly from the riding clothes he had worn to the boxing match. He walked down the stairs a half hour later in full morning dress: blue swallowtail coat of Bath superfine, buff waistcoat, cravat tied in the Osbaldistone, skin-tight pantaloons, and glossy hessians.

He entered the yellow saloon with a frown on his face, still worrying over the problem of what to do with Master Frederick, but at the sight of Lady Rennenord all thoughts of that irritating weakling left his head.

Lady Rennenord was a faultless, fashionable beauty. Chestnut-brown curls peeped out from beneath a saucy bonnet. Her eyes were large and brown and liquid under full, rather fleshy lids. Her nose was long and straight, and her mouth small enough to please the highest stickler. A riding costume of fine broadcloth in a dark lavender blossom color had been cut to make the most of her splendid figure. It had a high rolled collar, lapeled front, deep cape *á la pereline,* a broad belt secured in front with double clasp of steel, and a high ruff of double plaited muslin sloped to a point at the bosom. Light tan gloves and half shoes of lavender blossom kid completed the dazzling ensemble.

Mrs. Bellisle, her companion, was a hard-featured, mannish woman wearing a drab joseph and a flat hat. She looked so like a man and spoke in such a gruff, rude manner that it was assumed she was "Mrs." by courtesy rather than by marriage. No one could ever imagine that any man at one time had been brave enough to take Mrs. Bellisle to his bosom. And no one in the county could ever remember a Mr. Bellisle.

Dropping the earl a curtsy which involved a great deal of cracking joints, Mrs. Bellisle introduced Lady Rennenord.

When they were all seated, Mrs. Bellisle turned her protruding eyes on the earl. "What's this we hear of you being appointed guardian to old Armstrong's grandson?"

"I have said nothing," said the earl sweetly, "but no doubt my servants gossip."

"Is he a very *young* man?" asked Lady Rennenord, her voice pleasingly low and well modulated.

"He has eighteen years," said the earl, admiring the exquisite bloom on Lady Rennenord's cheeks. "He is unfortunately not very strong. I must admit I find myself at a loss as to what to do with the lad."

"Not your responsibility, Lord Berham,"

barked Mrs. Bellisle. "Send him to the military. Soon make a man of him."

The earl all at once thought of Freddie's childlike tear-stained face on the pillow upstairs and frowned.

"May I suggest, my lord," said Lady Rennenord quickly, "that you hire a tutor for the boy?"

"He is not exactly a boy, Lady Rennenord, although the delicacy and slightness of his figure make him appear one."

"I mean a tutor to engage his time, a man to take him shooting and instruct him in the other manly arts," explained Lady Rennenord, dropping her eyes so that her thick eyelashes fanned out over her cheeks.

"A good suggestion," said the earl. Lady Rennenord was beginning to please him more and more. There was a calmness about her, a suggestion of good breeding and good sense. He could not imagine her perpetrating a vulgar scene or, indeed, expressing any exaggeration of emotion. Her liquid brown eyes reflected a placid, well-ordered mind.

"I would be honored," went on the earl, "if both my charming visitors would stay to supper."

"That's very kind of you, Lord Berham," said Mrs. Bellisle promptly without waiting to see whether the arrangement suited her fair companion. In truth, Mrs. Bellisle was beginning to scent a romance. It would suit her very well to be rid of Clarissa Rennenord.

Clarissa was a relative several times removed.

Mrs. Bellisle had eagerly agreed to give the pretty widow house room, since the pretty widow came with a great deal of money, and, like quite a number of very rich people, Mrs. Bellisle was as clutch-fisted as a pauper. But Lady Rennenord's money could not outweigh the perpetual irritation of Lady Rennenord's good sense. Mrs. Bellisle was an autocratic lady who enjoyed bullying, but Clarissa made all the woman's forays in that direction seem like the wayward tantrums of a spoiled child. Furthermore, Lady Rennenord was not afraid of Mrs. Bellisle in the slightest.

The earl smiled and rang the bell. "Tell Master Frederick to join us here at six o'clock," he told his butler. "Come, ladies," he said, "and I will take you on a tour of my hothouses. My gardener, MacNab, has done wonders."

By the time the small party had returned to the yellow saloon to drink a glass of wine before supper, the earl found that he was enjoying himself. Lady Rennenord had been relaxing company. She knew a great deal about gardening and had even been able to point out to the redoubtable MacNab that his choice of colors for the central flower bed in the great lawn was a trifle garish, but she had added with a forgiving smile that since the seedlings had already been planted, there was little he could do about it short of digging everything up and starting again.

She professed herself eager to meet the earl's ward. "Delicate young men," she said, "often blossom under a woman's touch. My brother, I believe, would be just the man to find a tutor for the boy. You do not want a *learned* man but someone skilled in the gentlemanly arts."

"Well, we'll see what you make of Master Frederick." The earl smiled. "I believe he has arrived."

The door opened, and the slight figure of Freddie Armstrong edged around it.

He stood blinking in the light, his pale, delicate face overshadowed by his crown of thick red curls. He had violet circles under his eyes. The earl made the introductions. Freddie bowed to each lady and then took a chair in the corner and sat down. He was tolerably dressed in a morning coat of old-fashioned cut, and his cravat had been tied by his lordship's valet.

"We have been discussing your future, my boy," said the earl heartily. "Lady Rennenord had suggested I engage a tutor for you, someone who will coach you in the manly arts."

Was it a trick of the light, or did Freddie turn even paler?

"You certainly need building up," said Mrs. Bellisle. "Puny little thing, ain't you?"

"Now, Mrs. Bellisle," chided Lady Rennenord gently, "you must not embarrass the boy. A few weeks of exercise and country air will put him on his feet."

The earl smiled at her gratefully. Freddie

locked eyes with Lady Rennenord, and for one brief moment a flash of dislike flickered across his blue eyes.

Lady Rennenord's mouth tightened almost imperceptibly at the corners. "Yes, Master Frederick," she said sweetly, "by the time your tutor has finished with you, you will have the makings of a fine young man."

Freddie lowered his eyes.

From that moment on, he *hated* Lady Rennenord.

Chapter 2

The arrival of the tutor was hailed with relief by everyone except Master Frederick. Lady Rennenord's brother, Harry Struthers-Benton, had "turned up trumps," as he had put it, by finding a suitable individual.

The earl did not know that Mr. Struthers-Benton was hailed as a "loose screw" even by his intimates. On receiving his sister's request, he had enthusiastically forgotten about the whole thing until he had run across a certain Captain Cramble at a coffeehouse. Whether the brave captain had earned his rank at sea or in the military was hard to ascertain, but he claimed to be a past master at instructing young sprigs of the nobility in the manly arts, and the weak and shiftless Mr. Struthers-Benton had hired him on the spot.

Had the earl not been chafing to spend a little more time in Lady Rennenord's fair company and less in that of the seemingly ever-present Frederick, he might have cast a doubtful eye on Captain Cramble. But the responsibility of his guardianship was beginning to weigh heavy on him, and so he engaged the captain on the spot and turned Freddie over to him with a sigh of relief.

In the two weeks before the captain's arrival, Lady Rennenord had been a constant visitor. The weather had been unusually warm and mild, ideal for saunters in the grounds and pleasant dalliance. But where the earl and Lady Rennenord went, Master Frederick went too, his slight figure always at the earl's elbow. To tell the boy to run away would be to admit that his intentions towards Lady Rennenord were serious, and the earl did not yet want to commit himself.

Freddie was always courteous to his lady, but an undercurrent of animosity seemed to run between the two, spoiling the pleasure of the sunny days and tranquil evenings.

The earl had, however, found the boy stronger and more resilient than he had first thought. Master Freddie turned out to be a first-class horseman and an expert fencer. Still, the good captain would take the boy off his hands for a bit, thought the earl, so that he might make up his mind whether to propose to Lady Rennenord.

Her calm good sense intrigued him as he had never been intrigued before. Her liquid brown eyes rested on him with calm approval, but he longed to see them flash with passion. Nonetheless, he trusted her good sense so much that since she appeared to find no fault with the captain, it naturally followed that he should find nothing wrong with the man, either.

At first sight, Captain Cramble seemed a likeable sort, if a trifle too stout in the figure for such a master of sport. He had a very red face and pale eyes and reminded Freddie forcibly of Sheridan's caustic description of Dr. Arne, "two oysters in a plate of beet-root." He had great, heavy, plump hands and kept clapping Freddie heavily on the shoulder and calling him "my boy."

To Freddie's relief, however, the captain's instruction seemed to involve a great deal of talk and not very much action. As the earl appeared totally absorbed in Lady Rennenord's company, the captain soon settled down to a comfortable routine, not rising before noon, and then taking Master Frederick down to the local inn for "a glass or two," since the captain held to the maxim that every young sprig should learn to hold his wine.

These sessions were long and boring for Freddie, who did not care to drink much and emptied most of his glasses on the sawdust of the inn floor until such time as he should have to help his drunken tutor home.

But Freddie was miserable. He had grown very fond of his stern and handsome guardian and was sure the earl was about to make a disastrous mistake by proposing to Lady Rennenord. Lady Rennenord, Freddie decided, was a serpent in this Eden, a shrewd, hard, and calculating woman devoid of human kindness or warm feelings. Now he was tied to this wine sack of a tutor. Any complaint to the earl would, he was sure, be countered sweetly by Lady Rennenord.

One sunny day, when his tutor had passed out after a particularly lengthy session at the Old Bell, Berham's public house, Freddie went in search of his guardian.

He saw the gnarled figure of MacNab, the gardener, bent over a flower bed. "Where is my lord, MacNab?" he asked.

The gardener straightened up. "With my leddy, in the herb garden," he said sourly. "My leddy is no doubt telling my lord o' all the things I've done wrong."

Freddie flew off in the direction of the herb garden. It was enclosed in old sun-warmed gray walls at the back of the mansion. He stopped at the entrance, his hand to his mouth.

Lady Rennenord was wearing a bright green satin redingote with a spot pattern of darker green. On her glossy hair she sported a poke bonnet with curling ostrich plumes. She looked as if she had walked out of one of the glossy pages of *La Belle Assemblée*.

The earl was hatless and dressed in riding clothes. His head was bent over Lady Rennenord's hand. He was about to kiss it. The air was still and warm.

"No!" shouted Freddie.

Both heads jerked up. The earl strode towards Freddie, looking furious.

"No, what?" he demanded.

"I saw a great spider crawling up the back of Lady Rennenord's gown," said Freddie, blushing scarlet and improvising wildly.

Lady Rennenord did not even twist her head. She simply stood looking at Freddie with a wise little smile on her face.

"Are you sure?" demanded the earl, striding back to join Lady Rennenord.

"Oh, do not trouble, my lord," said Lady Rennenord. "I am persuaded the spider has disappeared. Don't you think so?" she demanded of Freddie, her eyes fixed on his flushed face.

"But it was *there!* I *saw* it!" said Freddie passionately.

"Where is Captain Cramble, young man?" demanded the earl.

"Asleep," said Freddie, suddenly cheerful. "So I am free to accompany you."

"Do you speak French?"

"Yes, my lord."

"Do you know the meaning of *de trop?*"

Freddie flushed. Lady Rennenord smiled a small, cool smile and studied a plant with great interest.

"Yes, my lord," mumbled Freddie, thinking desperately. "My lord," he said. "I think you really ought to take a look at Captain Cramble. He is breathing *most* peculiarly."

"Are you bamming me?" demanded the earl wrathfully. "First a mythical spider, and now the captain's breathing."

"Oh, no!" said Freddie, looking at him with limpid blue eyes. "And he is a most peculiar color."

"Excuse me, Lady Rennenord," said the earl

curtly. "This will not take long."

"Poor Lord Berham." Lady Rennenord laughed. "All the pains of marriage without any of the pleasures."

"Exactly," replied the earl, looking at her with a wicked gleam of amusement in his dark eyes.

He walked away with long strides, with Freddie running at his heels.

The earl strode into the captain's bedchamber. The curtains were closed, and the sound of strertorous breathing came from the bed.

The earl jerked open the curtains so that pale sun-light flooded the bedchamber. He turned and looked down at the captain. The captain's red face seemed even redder than ever, and his mouth was open. The earl bent his head and sniffed.

"Faugh!" he said, retreating a pace. "The man's drunk. How came this about?"

"The good captain was teaching me the manly arts of drinking," said Freddie with a sweetness worthy of Lady Rennenord.

The earl picked up a can of water from the toilet table and hurled the contents full in the captain's face. Then he turned to Freddie as the captain came awake, gasping and spluttering.

"Leave us," he snapped.

Freddie ran lightly down the stairs again, whistling cheerfully.

He went into the little-used drawing room and sat down at the pianoforte and proceeded to play a triumphant piece by Handel with great verve.

Suddenly he heard voices from the terrace outside, coming closer. He let his fingers rest on the keys and tilted his head to one side, listening.

"There was no need for you to call," came Lady Rennenord's voice. "I am too old to need a chaperone, and in truth, I have been dogged everywhere I go by Master Frederick."

"Perhaps it's just as well," came Mrs. Bellisle's barking voice. "A little difficulty in the path of love is a good thing. My lord has escaped marriage this long. He is not likely to propose without a great deal of thought. Perhaps Master Frederick is supplying the necessary frustration."

Freddie frowned thoughtfully at his fingers. Was this indeed the case? Would his beloved guardian propose to that fleshless, passionless female because of his, Freddie's, intervention?

He turned as the door opened and the earl walked in.

"Well, that is that," said his guardian. "I suppose I must excuse a small lapse such as occasional drunkenness. Captain Cramble was suitably abject and has promised it will not happen again. I have given him instructions to take you about the country for a bit. That will keep you from getting under my feet."

Freddie winced, and the earl surveyed him with some irritation. Master Frederick was much too nice in his feelings, too sensitive.

"I did not know you could play the piano-forte," said the earl abruptly. "Play something for me."

Freddie gave him an abrupt nod and began to play a Beethoven sonata, the liquid notes dropping one by one into the silence of the drawing room.

The earl sat down and stretched out his long, muscular legs, feeling the peace and beauty of the music seeping into his soul.

By George! The lad could play like an angel!

The pale gold light of the setting sun slanted through the long French windows that led onto the terrace.

The drawing room had not been used much since the earl's mother's death. Glass cases still held her treasured collection of Chinese carvings in jade and rock crystal, French and English enameled snuff-boxes, Russian bright *niello* work, and silver mugs. A full-length portrait of his mother hung above the fireplace, her eyes seeming to look down on the bright head of the boy bent over the keyboard.

Birds sang their evening song outside, and a breath of clean, warm, sweet air from the gardens moved the long Brussels lace curtains and sent them billowing out.

At last Freddie stopped, his thin, sensitive fingers resting on the keyboard.

The earl stared at the boy's bent head, inexpressibly moved by the beauty of the music, slightly in awe of this slim youth who could conjure up such magic.

He cleared his throat. He said brusquely, "Very good, my boy. You must play for Lady Rennenord."

"No!" said Freddie passionately, whirling about. "No, I will not!" His blue eyes were blazing in his white face.

The earl stood up. The obvious and correct thing to do was to fetch his riding crop and thrash Freddie for a piece of unpardonable insolence. Any of his peers would have done so without the slightest qualm. But he immediately knew he could not raise a hand to the boy, and this brought with it a feeling of impotence and rage.

"How dare you, you unpleasant, ill-mannered whelp!" he raged. "Lady Rennenord may shortly become my wife, and you will show her all due civility while you are under my roof!"

The earl looked awful in his rage, black eyes flashing, mouth set in a tight line.

Freddie ran forward and fell to his knees in front of him.

"Oh, I am sorry, my lord," he whispered. "I would not offend you for the world."

He raised blue, beseeching eyes to the earl's black, stormy ones.

The earl looked down at the boy curiously, his own eyes turning guarded, watchful and wary.

"What a pretty picture!" cried Lady Rennenord, sweeping through the French windows

36

with Mrs. Bellisle close behind. "Do not be too hard on Master Frederick. These lads will lie so."

"His tutor was drunk," said the earl harshly. "He did not lie. Go to your room, Frederick, and wait until I call you."

Freddie rushed from the drawing room, slamming the door noisily behind him.

"Where did your brother find Captain Cramble?" asked the earl.

Lady Rennenord looked at him in pretty puzzlement. "I confess I do not know. Is he not satisfactory? I feel a great deal of responsibility for him. I trust I have not brought some unsuitable person into your household."

"Perhaps I am too harsh," said the earl, but his smile was abstracted, and a crease of worry was between his brows.

To Lady Rennenord's well-concealed irritation, his lordship's strange abstraction continued throughout the rest of her visit.

"Where are we going?" demanded Freddie the next day. He was seated up in a gig beside his tutor, who was driving.

"Going to let you see a bit of excitement," said the captain, winking broadly. "Don't ask any questions. Spoil the surprise."

Freddie relapsed into a brooding silence. He had much to brood about. He had not been summoned to supper. A tray had been sent to him in his room.

Feeling he was going against orders, he had ventured downstairs in the morning, only to find that his guardian had left for the day. It was then that the captain had appeared, in high spirits, chuckling secretively over a promised treat which would "make Master Frederick stare."

The day was blustery and cold, with great gray and white clouds scudding across the sky. Winter had returned, and the long grass beside the road gleamed with unmelted frost.

Freddie felt very young and silly. Who was he to try to stop such a magnificent figure as the earl from proposing marriage to a respectable lady of good breeding? No doubt he was already down on one knee, begging for her hand in marriage. But after some thought, Freddie came to the conclusion that the earl was not the sort of man to bend his knee before anyone.

At least this expedition would pass some of the wearisome day, and with any luck, by the time evening fell, by some miracle the earl would still be a free man.

A flock of rooks sailed before the icy wind over the hard brown fields, and Freddie shivered as the gig jolted and rumbled along the country roads.

They had gone some distance when he espied the tall steeple of a church rising above the fields and, as they drew nearer, a cluster of houses.

A few more miles and Freddie realized they were approaching a biggish town.

"Where is this?" asked Freddie.

"Hardcaster," said his tutor. "Nearly there."

They rumbled through the cobbled streets of the town and drove into the yard of an inn called the Hare and Hounds.

The captain tossed a coin to an ostler. After they had climbed down and their gig was being led off to the stables, he tucked Freddie's slim arm in his own and led him out of the inn yard. "Time enough for a celebration when the fun is over," said the captain.

"Where are we going?" asked Freddie plaintively, horrified visions of seedy brothels beginning to dance before his eyes.

"Here!" said the captain triumphantly, coming to a halt before a peculiarly round-shaped building.

Freddie looked, and his heart sank to the worn soles of his patched boots.

"Does . . . does my lord know you are taking me to such a place?" he asked with a tremor in his voice.

"Course he does," said the captain heartily. " 'Take him about. Let him enjoy the things men enjoy.' That's what his lordship said."

Numbly, Freddie allowed himself to be led into the building.

It was a cockpit. The building was round, like a tower. Inside, it resembled the setting for an anatomy lecture. All around, the benches rose in tiers. In the middle was a round table on which the cocks had to fight.

To Freddie's increasing dismay, the captain had secured them places at the very front. Already the air seemed thick with gross anticipation of violence to come. Lords rubbed shoulders with bakers and butchers; men who looked as if they had barely enough to feed and clothe themselves were clutching fistfuls of notes, waiting for the betting to begin.

"Now, this here is very educational," said the captain, placing his mouth against Freddie's ear to make himself heard. "Some say this sport dates from the days of Themistocles. That general, it seems, was leading the Athenian army against the Persians when he observed two cocks fighting.

"He stopped the match, called a halt, and pointed out to his troops that the birds fought 'not for the gods of their country, nor for the monuments of their ancestors, nor glory, nor freedom, nor for their children; but for the sake of victory, and that one may not yield to the other.' It is a noble sport. Have you seen a cock-fight before?"

"Never," said Freddie.

The captain then plunged into a description of the preparation for a fighting cock for the ring, which seemed to Freddie to smack of witchcraft. It lacked only the eye of newt.

It took six weeks to bring a cock to his prime. For the first four days of that period he was fed with "the crumb of old manchet (fine wheaten roll) cut into square bits, at sun-rising, when the sun is in his meridian, and at sun-setting." His drinking water had to be from the coldest spring. After four days of this feeding, he was put to spar with another cock, with the cock's heels being covered with a sort of boxing glove.

Then you took both contestants and gave them "a diaphoretic or sweating" by burying them deep in a basket of straw after a dose of sugar candy, chopped rosemary, and fresh butter. Towards evening, you took them out of their "stoves" and "licked their eyes and head with your tongue."

Freddie was beginning to feel faint from the noise and jostling and bustling and the captain's hoarse voice shouting in his ear.

A basket on ropes swung above their heads. Anyone unable to pay his bets was put into the basket and hoisted high above the heads of the jeering crowd.

The cocks at last were brought forward, each concealed in a bag. The betting started before the "main," or match, began.

Everyone was betting feverishly.

At last the cocks were taken out of their bags. The birds had been trimmed for the fight, the crown of the head being snipped off close; the hackles, or neck feathers, being moderately shortened; and the tail feathers cut into the shape of a short fan.

Before Freddie's terrified eyes, both birds were fitted with the deadly "gaffes," or spurs.

These, some two inches in length, were curved like a surgeon's needle.

Freddie closed his eyes. Already, it seemed, he could see the carnage, the spurting blood.

One moment he was in his seat, dizzy and faint, and the next he was up on the table, his arms spread, crying, "Stop! Oh, please, stop."

There was utter and complete silence.

"How can you, in the name of God and all his angels," said Freddie, tears starting to his eyes, "allow such a disgusting and detestable sport to take place?"

There was a great jeering roar of derision.

"Put 'im in the basket and let's be done with 'im," shouted one voice, louder than the rest.

This was greeted with a roar of approval, and hands reached out to seize Freddie.

Freddie drew his small, short sword and waved it about, his face flushed and determined.

A young exquisite leapt nimbly onto the cockpit table, drew his own sword, and faced Freddie. "Let's see what type of fighting cock you are, young fellow," he sneered.

Eyes glittering with unshed tears, Freddie gamely squared up to his opponent. Betting started as everyone began to lay odds on the outcome of the contest. Captain Cramble, who had been about to flee in case he ended up in the basket with Freddie, sat down again and promptly began laying his bets. He had seen Freddie's expertise with the small sword. Although Freddie's opponent was taller and stronger and had the longer reach, the captain was confident that Freddie would acquit himself well.

The fight began. Freddie lunged and parried, nimbly keeping his footing on the small stage afforded by the table, dodging time and again under his opponent's arm.

Tense, ugly, and flushed with excitement, the tiers of spectators waited for first blood.

Into the tense and strained silence a shot rang out like a clap of thunder.

"Hold hard," cried a loud voice. "The next man that moves will get his brains blown out."

The Earl of Berham, smoking dueling pistol in one hand, vaulted lightly over the heads of the spectators and down onto the table.

Freddie looked at him. The young man's face was ashen, his lips were white, and his blue eyes were blurred with tears.

"Sir," said Freddie weakly, "I was trying to stop the cockfight." Then he collapsed in a dead faint.

The earl swung him over one shoulder and darted lightly up over the benches before the stunned audience had time to make a move.

His groom was standing outside the cockpit, holding the reins of a team of matched bays harnessed to a racing curricle. The earl dumped Freddie like a sack of potatoes on the seat, called to the groom to stand away from the horses' heads, and set off, hell for leather, out of Hardcaster.

When he was a mile out of town, he finally reined in his horses and looked grimly down at Freddie, who had recovered from his faint and was gazing at him with wide, frightened eyes.

"You have some explaining to do, Master Frederick," said the earl harshly. "Or should I say . . . Miss Frederica?"

Chapter 3

"How did you find me?" Freddie asked in a low voice.

The earl turned his head and told his groom to walk down the road a little and leave them to have their conversation in private. Then he said, "MacNab, the gardener, saw a bill dropping from the captain's gig as you drove off. He found it advertised a cockfight in Hardcaster. He guessed that I would not approve and sent a messenger to Mrs. Bellisle's to tell me the news. I came as fast as I could. Had you been the young man you pretend to be, I should simply have waited until the captain returned with you. I disapprove of cockfighting. But I had guessed you were a girl and was frightened you might betray your sex. So I had to travel as fast as I could. The question is, Where is the real Frederick Armstrong?"

Freddie twisted her fingers and gave a little sigh. "There is no Frederick Armstrong. I am Frederica Armstrong, granddaughter of Colonel Armstrong."

"But why this masquerade? And why did that parcel of lawyers go along with this farce?"

"My grandfather never told anyone I was a

girl," sighed Freddie. "My father died three months before I was born. My mother died in childbirth. So, you see, apart from two servants who are now dead, there was no one to contest grandfather's claim that I was a boy. He made me wear boy's clothes and had tutors teach me to ride and fence."

"I have heard of some eccentrics wanting a son so much that they will almost turn a girl into one. Was that the reason for this folly?"

Freddie shook her red head. "No, Grandfather had very odd views. He thought women had a dangerous life. He did not think he would be alive to see me wed, and so he said it would be better for me to be a boy. He said unprotected women were easy prey to the lusts of men. He told me I must understand these were the hard facts of life. He even took me to a brothel once to . . . to observe.

"It was all very odd," Freddie went on, turning a pair of ingenuous blue eyes up to the earl's brooding face. "I would never have thought that ladies could behave in such an undignified manner. As a matter of fact, I was quite sick."

The earl looked straight ahead between his horses' ears. "If your grandfather were alive," he said in measured tones, "I would shoot him for doing such a thing to an innocent girl."

"Oh, he was very kindly," explained Freddie. "He simply feared for my future welfare."

"He must have been some kind of a satyr himself," the earl pointed out caustically, "to think that all men were consumed by base lust. Furthermore, did it not cross his mind that he should hire some female companion or governess or have you adopted by some lady of quality?"

"No. You see, he had alienated nearly everybody, apart from the vicar, that is, and the vicar thought I was a boy and would have been monstrous shocked to find out that was not the case."

"Did none of your tutors guess the identity of your sex?"

"No," sighed Freddie, "because I was . . . I am," she added with a rueful look at her own slim figure, "very boyish in appearance. Of course, when I was younger, there was nothing really to wonder about. Now, of course, that I am grown, I began to appear effeminate. My voice is quite low, but it is uncomfortable to wear a binder at all times, especially in hot weather."

"A binder?"

Freddie flushed and made a fleeting gesture with one hand towards her flattened bosom.

"Now what am I to do with you?" sighed the earl as Freddie's blue eyes filled with tears. "No, don't cry," he said gently. "I shall not berate you for a circumstance which was none of your making. But only see the difficulties of my position. Were the fact to come out that you are a girl, you would be compromised. No one would believe I had not known."

"If I loved someone," said Freddie, twisting a handkerchief in her fingers, "I would believe him without question."

"Perhaps you are right. I need the help of a lady. I shall speak to Lady Rennenord on my return."

"I wouldn't do that," said Freddie quickly. "She will think the very worst."

"Look, young man, I mean, young lady, it has been quite obvious to me that you have taken Lady Rennenord in dislike. You will treat her with the utmost civility for my sake, if not for your own. For your information, I was about to propose marriage to her when my servant burst in with the intelligence of your visit to the cockfight."

"I would not have her know," said Freddie, turning her face away.

A broad river meandered through the fields beside the road. Freddie watched the reflection of the full-bottomed clouds scudding across its surface, quivering and distorted by the ripples of the dying wind. The earl watched Freddie.

Her red hair blazed and dimmed and blazed again in the fleeting checkerboard of sun and shadow. She had not been cursed with a redhead's usual pale and freckled complexion but had a rose-leaf cheek and vivid blue eyes, their long black lashes tipped with gold. He was amazed that he had ever considered her a boy. She looked at that moment, even with her averted head, extremely feminine and vulnerable.

Her odd, husky voice spoke again: "What will become of me?"

"I think I must consult Lady Rennenord," said the earl quietly. "I know you do not like her, but have you considered it is because you have not been in the way of female company?"

No answer.

"Nonetheless," said the earl after a pause, "I must consult her, if only because, as my intended bride, she should not be kept from anything that concerns my life. The servants, too, must be told. They are loyal to me and will not gossip."

"They will all stare at me and . . ."

"I shall address them while you are not present," replied the earl. "You may leave matters to me."

The earl called to his groom, who was waiting discreetly at a short distance down the road, and then picked up the reins. Freddie clutched at the side of the curricle and wondered miserably what was in store for her. If Lady Rennenord had any say in her future, Freddie was sure it would be something unpleasant.

By the time the tall chimneys of Berham Court began to appear above the trees, Freddie was beginning to feel considerably more cheerful. She had decided that Lady Rennenord would be so shocked by the masquerade that she would have nothing further to do with the earl.

"When did you discover I was not a boy?" she asked shyly.

The earl slowed his team while he wondered what to say. The correct answer was that his own feelings towards Freddie when she knelt in front of him had alerted him to the fact that she was a girl.

Instead he replied, "Because you are too pretty to be a young man."

"Really!" Freddie flushed to the roots of her hair with pleasure and put a coquettish little hand up to pat her curls.

The earl glanced at her and smiled. "There are some of my mother's clothes in the attic. I shall tell the servants to alter some of the gowns for you as a temporary measure."

"Can't I wear these?" asked Freddie, indicating her shabby suit.

"Don't you *want* to wear pretty things?" countered the earl as the carriage swept around in front of Berham Court.

"I'm afraid," said Freddie in a low voice. "I don't know how to behave like a woman."

"Oh, I think you do," said the earl, remembering the way she had flushed with pleasure at his compliment. "Now, run up to your room and I will tell the servants of your masquerade."

An hour later, the earl was back out on the road again, driving towards Mrs. Bellisle's home to enlist the help of Lady Rennenord.

He was looking forward to placing the problem of Freddie before her. He could almost hear her calm, sensible voice smoothing away his difficulties.

The servants had been remarkably calm over the announcement of Freddie's sex. The earl would have been amazed could he have seen the scene in his servants' hall at that moment.

One of the housemaids had a country swain who had been present at the cockfight and had ridden hard to Berham Court to relate the gossip of Master Frederick's brave stand. Hard on the heels of this had come his lordship's summons to the great hall and consequent announcement that Master Frederick was in fact Miss Frederica Armstrong. The earl had painted a sympathetic picture of Freddie's strange upbringing. Freddie was now the heroine of the day in the servants' hall.

"I could tell Miss Armstrong was a real lady," sighed Cook sentimentally. "Such kind considerate ways, she has. Always a thank you and a bit of praise. Not like some I could mention who thinks they're going to be mistress here."

"I think my lord is going to propose to Lady Rennenord," said MacNab gloomily.

"Well, it's a shame," said Cook. "My lord really should marry Miss Frederica, that he should. She needs an older man to guide her. And if that Lady Rennenord has her say, Miss Frederica won't be allowed to stay at Berham Court. That woman is a devil in garnet!"

Blissfully unaware that his intended bride was already highly unpopular with his staff, the earl rode on with a mounting feeling of anticipation.

He would tell Clarissa Rennenord about poor Freddie's predicament and ask her advice. Perhaps when they were married, they could have the townhouse redecorated and give Freddie a Season in London.

A nagging little voice somewhere inside was trying to tell the earl that his beloved had not been precisely efficient when it came to recommending a tutor for Freddie. The earl had left instructions that should the captain dare to return to Berham Court, he was to be sent packing immediately. If he did not return, his trunks were to be sent to his address in London.

But Mrs. Bellisle's home was very near. The day was cold and sunny. Soon he would see Lady Rennenord and watch her calm, elegant movements and study that tranquil face and try to guess the mysterious passions and secrets it held.

"He's back," said Lady Rennenord crossly, looking out the window and down the short drive to where the earl's curricle could be seen swinging round from the road between the gateposts.

Mrs. Bellisle looked up from the magazine she was reading. "I suppose I must absent myself again." She sighed. "Do you really think he means to propose, Clarissa?"

"Of course he does," said Lady Rennenord. "He would have done had not his servant come bursting in with the news that that boy, Freddie, had gone to a cockfight. The way Lord Berham ran out of the house, you would think the boy was about to be hanged instead of attending a sporting event."

"Get rid of that brat as soon as you become Lady Berham," said Mrs. Bellisle, "or you will have no peace."

"Oh, I intend to," replied Lady Rennenord sweetly.

Mrs. Bellisle managed to escape from the morning room a bare minute before the earl was ushered in.

Lady Rennenord curtsied low and resumed her seat, picking up a piece of embroidery and bending her head over it. She hoped she presented a suitably domestic and wifely picture.

But the earl did not sit down. He started to pace up and down the small room. Lady Rennenord raised her fine eyes and looked at him with well-concealed exasperation. Would the man never get to the point?

At last the earl swung round and faced her. "There is something I must tell you," he said abruptly.

"Yes, my lord?" asked Lady Rennenord while she surreptitiously edged a footstool a few inches in his direction so that it would be in a more convenient position when he fell on one knee to propose to her.

"It's about Freddie," said the earl. Lady Rennenord quickly lowered her eyes to her sewing again.

"He . . . damn . . . *she* is a girl. Colonel Armstrong was such an eccentric that he brought her up as a boy. He willed her to me, probably not knowing my father was dead and thinking he was entrusting her to the safe care of an equally old man."

Lady Rennenord spasmodically clutched the piece of embroidery and pricked her finger. She looked down at the small bubble of blood and carefully wiped it away with a wisp of handkerchief. The red-headed minx, she thought furiously. Eccentric old grandfather, indeed! It's the result of a well-hatched plot. The doxy has been under his roof without a chaperone. He'll need to marry her. What does he want, my blessing? The fool!

The earl's voice went on. "The girl has not been compromised. My servants will not gossip, and of course, I trust your discretion implicitly." He looked at her anxiously, but her head was bent over the crumpled piece of embroidery.

"I trust *Miss* Freddie came to no harm at the cockpit?" she eventually asked in a thin, dry voice.

"I arrived in time," he said, sitting down opposite her. "She was fighting a duel with a man almost twice her size, right in the middle of the cockpit table. It seems she tried to stop the main. I shudder to think what would have happened to her had I not been there. Captain Cramble has been dismissed."

"That seems a trifle harsh," said Lady Rennenord, still not raising her eyes. "He thought he was taking a young man."

"It was no place for a young man, either," said the earl severely. "It is a savage and barbarous sport."

"I am sorry my help turned out to be useless," said her ladyship, raising her eyes at last. They were calm and undisturbed, reflecting none of the irritation, jealousy, and exasperation underneath.

"Ah, no!" said the earl warmly. "You did your best. You are not to be blamed. As a matter of fact, I stand badly in need of your help and advice. What am I to do with Miss Frederica Armstrong?"

Lady Rennenord smoothed the crumpled piece of embroidery on her lap and carefully picked out the needle.

If she had replied promptly, if she had said she would do anything to help, the earl would have proposed marriage and then told her his idea of giving Freddie a Season. But that deliberate little gesture suddenly reminded him of a governess he had had when he was little, who had performed the same little deliberate movements without looking at him just before she was about to say something very unpleasant.

And so he waited patiently, trying to banish that irritating memory from his mind.

Lady Rennenord was thinking things out very carefully. He must look on her as a future wife or he would not have asked for her help. She had a sudden picture of what Freddie might look like dressed as a girl, with her flaming curls and blue eyes. Yes, Freddie must be got rid of, and quickly. At least he obviously did not think he had to marry the girl.

"There is a seminary at Lamstowe, on the coast," said Lady Rennenord, marshaling all her resources and turning a calm, sweet gaze on the earl. She held up her hand as he would have spoken. "I know what you are about to say, Lord Berham — that Miss Armstrong is too old for a seminary. But not for this one. It deals in training young ladies of good family in manners and dress. Young ladies of all ages. Several families who have experienced difficulties with their daughters have found that two years at this seminary have been very beneficial. It is run by the Misses Hope, two maiden ladies of breeding and skill.

"The seminary is pleasantly situated on the cliffs outside of town. The climate is salubrious and bracing. I think the sooner Miss Armstrong is conveyed there, the better. Once she has been trained in the social graces, why, then she will be ready to make her debut in society, should you wish."

"A very good suggestion," said the earl, although there was a little crease of worry between his brows. He did not know quite what he had hoped for. Perhaps that Lady Rennenord herself would volunteer to take Freddie under her wing. Of course, he could propose marriage on the spot, and that would certainly alter the situation. On the other hand, he himself could not school Freddie. He would be free of the irksome responsibility of looking after the girl. So . . .

"Very well," he said. "Perhaps if you could furnish me with the address? Good."

"It would not be proper for you to travel to Lamstowe with Miss Armstrong," said Lady Rennenord. "It might occasion comment. Better to send her away as soon as possible."

"I must say, you are taking it very well." The earl smiled. "I was afraid you might be shocked."

"Not I." Lady Rennenord smiled back. Furious, said her inner voice, but not shocked. "You have been the victim of a cruel trick."

"I think it is Miss Frederica who has been the victim of a cruel trick," said the earl.

There was a little silence. Mrs. Bellisle could be heard moving about upstairs. Lady Rennenord cleared her throat with a delicate little cough.

"Have you anything further you wish to ask me, Lord Berham?"

Now was the time to propose, yet he found he could not. Perhaps he felt guilty over the thought of Freddie's banishment so soon to come. When the girl was packed off, he could settle down to his courtship with an easy conscience.

He shook his head, thanked her again, and made his good-byes.

Mrs. Bellisle came running into the morning room a few moments later at the sound of breaking china. Lady Rennenord was sitting over her embroidery. A Dresden figure lay smashed on the floor over by the window.

"What happened?" asked Mrs. Bellisle, ringing the bell for a servant to clear away the pieces.

"It must have fallen," said Clarissa Rennenord, tranquilly threading a needle.

Mrs. Bellisle looked puzzled. It looked as if the figure which had been on the mantelpiece had been hurled against the opposite wall by a furious hand.

"Did he ask you?" she demanded instead.

"Not yet," said Lady Rennenord. "But he will."

Chapter 4

Freddie did not learn of the plans for her future until four days after the earl returned from his visit to Lady Rennenord. She barely saw the earl, since he appeared to be absent most of the time and took his meals in his study. He had decided against dressing her in women's clothes despite the fact that the housemaids had altered several of his late mother's dresses. "Better to keep up the masquerade," he said, until it was time for Freddie to leave.

"Leave when, and for where?" Freddie asked the servants anxiously. But they could only shake their heads and say that a messenger had been sent off by the earl and was expected to be back within four days. That it was something to do with Miss Frederica's future was all they knew.

The earl parried all Freddie's anxious questions by simply saying, "Wait and see."

But at last he had a reply by hand from the Misses Hope. They would be delighted, they wrote, to school the earl's ward.

Attached to the letter was a handbill lauding the establishment and stating the fees, and another sheet of paper listing the clothes it would be necessary for Freddie to bring. The Misses Hope said that by fortuitous chance they had a vacancy at that very moment.

The earl put down the letter with a little sigh. He could not rid himself of a nagging feeling of guilt. He had persuaded himself that he was avoiding Freddie merely to satisfy the conventions, but he was really afraid of becoming too attached to the girl. He admired her spirit and was heartily sorry for the odd and lonely life she had led.

He had not seen Lady Rennenord since that day when she had offered her good advice, and absence was definitely making the earl's heart grow very fond. She had left to visit friends in a neighboring county and was not expected back for another two weeks. Mrs. Bellisle had gone with her.

Lady Rennenord had in fact guessed that a separation from her was just what the earl needed to bring him up to the mark.

With another little sigh, he rang the bell and ordered Miss Frederica to be sent to him.

In a short time Freddie came bouncing in. The earl looked with disfavor at her shabby suit of morning clothes.

"It's bad enough, your being dressed in men's clothes," he said severely, "but need they be quite so shabby? Your grandfather was a rich man."

Freddie grinned. "He did not believe in wasting money on clothes," she said. "He believed one should wear one's clothes until they fell to bits. Oh, my lord, I am so glad you are not angry with me anymore!"

"I never was angry with you," said the earl. "Sit down, Frederica. We must discuss your future. You cannot stay here with me. It is not conventional."

"Perhaps you have some female relative who might chaperone me," said Freddie eagerly. "I have been thinking about it quite a lot and . . ."

The earl shook his head. He picked up the letter from the seminary. In a clear, precise voice, he outlined Freddie's future, keeping his eyes fixed on the letter, sensing her dismay. At last he looked up. Freddie looked back at him, her face completely devoid of expression.

Freddie wanted to shout and scream and rave. She wanted to throw herself on her knees and beg him not to send her away. But since he had already agreed to this arrangement — Freddie was in no doubt that it was Lady Rennenord's idea — he obviously did not want her around. If he had, he would have made arrangements to find a chaperone for her. A hard lump rose up in Freddie's throat, but she kept her face well schooled.

"When have I to leave?" she asked, her voice sounding strange in her own ears.

"In a few days," he said. "The sooner the better." Freddie flinched, but he did not notice, for he had bent his head over the letter again.

"You will feel strange at first, but you will

have female friends for the first time in your life. You will learn how to act like a lady. When you have finished your schooling, it will be time to consider your London debut. I will likely be married by then, and my wife will be able to help you make your come-out."

"I do not think I ever want to get married," said Freddie, watching the earl's bent head, the strong lines of his face, his firm mouth.

"It's natural you should feel that way at the moment," he said. "You have been brought up to think all men lustful beasts. It will take you some time to adjust."

"I don't think *all* men so," Freddie replied falteringly.

"No? Well, I hope you don't include me in that category."

"Oh, *no!*"

"Thank you. You are going to be very busy in the next few days being fitted for a wardrobe. Fortunately, the seminary states they wish you to wear plain and simple gowns.

"I am afraid my female staff will need to fashion them for you. It would occasion too much comment were they made anywhere else. Can you sew?"

Freddie shook her head.

She stared at him solemnly, and for a moment he thought he saw loneliness and fear in her eyes. But the next minute she was saying cheerfully, "Shall I see much of you before I leave?"

"I have much to attend to about the estates,"

said the earl. "And our situation is delicate. I do not wish to entertain anyone here until you have left."

He stood up, indicating that the interview was at an end.

"Where is this seminary?" asked Freddie.

"At Lamstowe. On the coast. On the cliffs."

Freddie brightened. "I have never seen the sea, my lord. And how long will I be gone?"

"Two years is suggested."

"Two years!"

"It will pass very quickly. Of course, you may return on holidays and things like that," he added.

"And will I travel to this seminary alone?"

"You will use my traveling carriage. The coachman, grooms, and outriders will go with you. I will find some suitable female to accompany you. And now, if that is all . . ."

"Yes," said Freddie bleakly.

She studied his handsome face for a long moment, searching for some sign of affection. Then, with a little sigh, she turned and left the room.

After a week of being turned and pinned and fitted, Freddie was declared ready to depart. All her spare moments she had haunted the rooms and grounds of Berham Court, looking for the earl, but he was never anywhere to be found. The servants were very quiet about Miss Frederica's forthcoming exile to Lamstowe. It was not for them to criticize their master's decision. But privately each and every one thought it was very hard on the girl and laid the blame for the choice of a seminary fairly and squarely on Lady Rennenord's absent shoulders.

The housemaids who had been engaged to make Freddie's wardrobe had fulfilled the seminary's request for "plain, serviceable clothes with nothing included to excite Vanity" but had rebelled when it came to Freddie's outfit for traveling.

They had found a riding habit which had belonged to the earl's mother and had set about refitting it to Freddie's slim figure. It was made of rich cloth velvet, double-breasted and tightly fitted at the waist. The revers were of scarlet and white silk, a dramatic contrast to the midnight blue of the cloth. It was to be worn with a muslin cravat and a dashing felt bonnet with the crown bound with gold cord tassels.

Freddie had given up any hope of seeing the earl before she left, but he was waiting for her in the great hall as she descended the stairs in all the glory of her dashing riding suit.

He looked at her long and wonderingly, amazed that he had ever thought her a boy, even for a moment. Her bosom, freed from its confining binder, was revealed at last by the trim, well-cut bodice of the habit. Her glossy red curls peeped out from beneath the brim of her bonnet.

Freddie came down towards him and then stood looking up at him shyly.

"I feared I would not see you again, my lord," she said.

"I would not let you go away without saying good-bye," he said. "I have brought your chaperone."

Freddie looked nervously beyond him to where a tall woman stood in the shadows of the hall, half fearing to see Lady Rennenord.

"Miss Manson is a retired schoolmistress," said the earl. "She is very discreet and trustworthy, and she will engage to see you delivered safely."

Freddie was led forward. She made a low bow, having not yet managed to learn how to curtsy.

Miss Manson was a tall, gaunt, forbidding-looking woman wearing a drab walking dress and a depressed bonnet. She had faded light blue eyes and a large beaky nose which seemed to be pushed to one side. She opened her mouth in a smile, baring strong yellow teeth.

Freddie nervously murmured her thanks to Miss Manson for electing to accompany her. Miss Manson replied that it was her pleasure. Then all three stood awkwardly.

"Well," said the earl at last. "The carriage awaits, Frederica." He held out his hand and gave Freddie's gloved hand a polite shake.

To the earl's surprise, all the servants had assembled outside to say good-bye to Freddie. Some of the housemaids were weeping openly. The tall liveried footmen stood in a row on either side of the entrance, forming a sort of guard of honor.

Freddie approached the coach, obviously trying to curb her mannish stride. The sun shone brightly. Golden daffodils on the lawns were bending before a brisk wind.

One foot on the step of the carriage, Freddie hesitated and then impulsively swung around. She ran to the housekeeper, a stout lady called Mrs. Deighton. "Oh, I trust you will keep well," she said breathlessly, "and that you will not be sorely troubled by the rheumatism now that winter is over. And Rose, do not cry so. My lord says I may return on holidays, so I will see you all again quite soon."

And so Freddie ran from one to the other, shaking hands and giving them all her best wishes.

The earl thought uneasily that it was as well his beloved was not present to witness this rather shockingly democratic scene, although he had to admit that Freddie seemed to have the knack of being on easy terms with his servants without losing her young dignity one whit.

Freddie then bowed to the earl. "Thank you for your hospitality and great kindness, my lord," she said in a voice that wavered a little.

"It will be Easter soon," said the earl. "I will send for you then. So you see, you will not be away from us for so very long."

"Oh, *thank* you!" said Freddie. Then she thought that the earl might be engaged to Lady Rennenord by then, and a shadow crossed her face.

Miss Manson had already settled herself in the coach. Freddie climbed in. The footmen slammed the door. The coachman cracked his whip. The servants gave Freddie three loud huzzas.

Then, as the coach was only a little way down the drive, Freddie rapped on the roof and called, "Stop! Oh, please stop!"

The coachman slowed his team to a halt.

Freddie tore open the door of the carriage and hurtled out. She ran full tilt back to where the earl was standing on the steps, threw her arms about him, and kissed him on the cheek.

Then, with a little gasp, she swung about, ran back to the coach, and jumped in.

The earl stood for a long time, his hand to his cheek, looking after the departing coach until it had disappeared from view.

Freddie sat, unseeing, watching the passing countryside through a blur of tears. Then she realized that there were certain compensations in being a girl. She could cry openly.

Miss Manson made no comment as Freddie choked and sobbed, until Freddie gave a particularly large and noisy gulp. Miss Manson said, "Please *don't*, Miss Armstrong. You must not distress yourself like this. I am very susceptible to grief. My nerves were never strong." And with that, the chaperone pulled out an enormous handkerchief and burst into tears as well.

Freddie blew her nose hurriedly. "It is all right, Miss Manson. I am quite recovered.

Please do not refine on it too much. I am a trifle exercised with the natural distress of leaving a home I had come to love."

"Then I am cheerful now," said Miss Manson, her tears disappearing as if someone had turned off a tap.

"Did Lady Rennenord suggest you as a suitable chaperone?" asked Freddie, looking at her strange companion with some curiosity.

"Yes," said Miss Manson. "I was most surprised and gratified. I am retired, you know, although I am not precisely *old*. I taught at the Berham Seminary for Young Ladies, which closed last year owing to lack of pupils. Lady Rennenord had heard I was very strict."

"And are you?"

"Oh, yes. Very," said Miss Manson with an awful frown.

Freddie giggled. "I do not think you are strict at all!"

"But I can appear to be. In fact, I am quite good at it. But since we are to be companions on this journey, it does not seem a very sensible thing to be strict when there is nothing that I can see to be strict *about*."

"Do you know Lady Rennenord well?" asked Freddie, forgetting a little of her distress at being banished from Berham Court in her interest in her companion.

"Quite well. Mrs. Bellisle brought her several times to one of our tea parties. I am one of the leading members of the Society for Indigent

Berham Gentlewomen. She very kindly gave us some clothes and a little lecture on the value of humility."

"Really," said Freddie dryly.

"I admire her," said Miss Manson earnestly. "Such a calm and wise exterior, such an *enamel* of wisdom covering an inside of stupidity and petty spite."

"My dear Miss Manson. You are extremely and brutally frank. What makes you think I should not be outraged at your cruel remarks?"

"Because you do not like Lady Rennenord at all," said Miss Manson simply. "How could you? It was her idea you should be sent away. She hoped to marry Lord Berham. You were bitterly distressed at leaving. I thought a few nasty remarks about Lady Rennenord would raise your spirits."

Freddie gave a gurgle of laughter. "You are perceptive, Miss Manson. Lady Rennenord has not been very long in the district, and yet you seem to have gauged her character very well. What of Mrs. Bellisle?"

"A bully, pure and simple. But quite harmless, unless, of course, one has the misfortune to be one of her servants."

"And . . . and Lord Berham?"

"A fine and handsome gentleman. Upright, honest, charming, and *much* too good for Lady Rennenord."

"Miss Manson," said Freddie, "I think I love you."

"Now, that's a pleasant thing," exclaimed Miss Manson with a surprisingly girlish laugh. "I declare you will be forgetting you are not a young man anymore."

"Ah, you heard about my masquerade."

"Of course. Lady Rennenord was quite shocked."

"I hope she did not tell anyone else. I would not like Lord Berham to think he had been compromised."

"Neither would Lady Rennenord. It stands to reason, since she wishes to marry him herself."

"Did . . . did she say so?"

"She talked about what she planned to do to Berham Court when she became mistress there, and so . . ."

"I wish there was some way I could stop her," said Freddie.

"Perhaps Lord Berham will come to his senses," said Miss Manson comfortably. "You see, even very worldly and experienced men such as Lord Berham who have escaped marriage for so long are suddenly struck with an impulse to marry, and that is when they usually fall in love with perfectly unsuitable females. In his normal state of mind, Lord Berham would not look in her direction. But he is not married *yet*."

"She will have him," said Freddie gloomily. "She is a very determined woman."

"Are you — forgive me for the personal nature of the question — are you in love with him yourself?"

"I?" said Freddie, startled. "My dear Miss Manson, I admire Lord Berham with all my heart, but I see him very much as the kind and generous guardian he is. Besides, I am too young and not yet feminine enough to catch his eye, should such a ridiculous notion enter my head!"

"I think you look very well," said Miss Manson. "At least you are fashionably and adequately dressed for the weather. I do not approve of the latest fashions. Seminudity seems to be the desired state. All these loose flowing garments are very dangerous. So easy to catch on fire. It is the same with all those ridiculous fashions for children; girls with fluttering ribbons and boys with sashes. It reminds one of that beautiful cautionary poem:

Little Willy in his brand new sash
Fell in the fire and was burned to ash.
Later on the night grew chilly,
But nobody came to poke poor Willy."

Freddie laughed with delight. How furious Lady Rennenord would be if she could hear the seemingly prim schoolmistress now!

Freddie enjoyed the journey to Lamstowe more than she had enjoyed anything in her life before. It was hard to remember that Miss Manson was a middle-aged spinster. She chattered and laughed like a young girl. Freddie began to entertain high hopes of the girls she would meet at the seminary. Then she began to dream of turning into an elegant young lady so that the earl might be proud of her. And maybe, if she prayed very hard indeed, he would not marry Lady Rennenord.

Lamstowe was at last reached. They had stayed the night at a posting house on the outskirts so that they would be able to arrive fresh and well rested early the following morning.

Freddie had long dreamed of her first glimpse of the sea, imagining it spread out blue and glittering, dotted with white sails. But it was a sullen, heaving, restless gray expanse that met her eyes as the carriage rolled along the road on the top of the cliffs above the town of Lamstowe, which crouched at their feet in a jumble of slate-roofed houses.

A chill wind blew from the east, and the lowering clouds threatened rain. A few sheep cropped at the rough heathland which stretched out on the side of the road from the sea.

"It is not a very welcoming prospect," said Freddie. "And it is an odd place for a seminary, so isolated, so far from the town."

"The town seems to be in the nature of a large fishing village," replied Miss Manson. "The seminary would need to be housed in a fairly large mansion, I should think. And there was probably not a large enough house in the town itself."

Freddie lowered the carriage window and stuck her head out. A large building rose above a cluster of stunted trees at the next bend in the road.

"I think we are nearly there." Freddie sank back in her seat. "There is a house up ahead."

A pang of unease assailed her. She had pictured a sunny mansion with spacious gardens.

The coach swung off the road between two tall gateposts. "Yes," murmured Freddie. "Journey's end."

The carriage plowed up the uneven surface of the short drive and came to a halt outside the seminary.

Both ladies climbed stiffly down and stood looking up at the house.

It was all very gothic. The wind howled mournfully through the trees, and somewhere a broken shutter banged and cracked.

One of the grooms rang the bell. After a few moments the door was opened by a grim-faced maid who ushered the ladies into a dark hall which smelled of disinfectant and cabbage water. The air was chill and damp.

Freddie began to wonder hysterically if she was to be the only pupil. There was no sound at all but the wind in the chimneys and that restless bang-bang-banging of the shutters.

They followed the maid through the shadowy hall. She pushed open a door at the far end, bobbed a curtsy, and left.

Two ladies rose as Freddie and Miss Manson entered the room. This, then, must be the Misses Hope.

They introduced themselves as Miss Mary Hope and Miss Cassandra Hope. Miss Mary was tall and thin and dressed in rustling black silk and a large turban. She had an air of perpetual surprise caused by her arched brows and prissed-up mouth. She looked as if someone had just shoved something nasty-smelling under her nose.

Miss Cassandra was small and plump and dressed in girlish sprigged muslin. She had made an effort to fight the cold of the mansion by wrapping herself around in a number of shawls and stoles and scarves. She had an olive complexion and the shadow of a mustache above her surprisingly full and red mouth. She wore an elaborate lace cap on her head.

Freddie moved a little closer to Miss Manson.

"We are pleased to welcome you, Miss Armstrong," said Miss Mary. She turned to Miss Manson and inclined her head. "You may go."

"Go?" said Freddie, startled. "But Miss Manson has come a long way. Surely it is possible to offer her some refreshment, at least."

"You are very forward, Miss Armstrong," said Miss Cassandra meditatively. "But we shall soon correct that."

Miss Manson took a deep breath. "Before I leave," she said. "I would like to see Miss Armstrong's room, I would like to see the kitchens, and I would like to talk to some of the teachers."

Miss Mary went and held open the door. "You are nothing more than a servant, Miss Manson," she said awfully. "Furthermore, you

74

are presumptuous. We have received instructions from Lord Berham. You are to deliver Miss Armstrong into our care and leave immediately."

Freddie ran and threw her arms about Miss Manson. "Oh, do as they say," she whispered. "Only remember that I shall be home very soon, and I will *beg* Lord Berham not to leave me here."

Miss Manson hugged her back. "I do not like this place at all," she said in a low voice. "I will return to Berham and get my lord to send the carriage for you as soon as possible."

"Miss Armstrong!" said Miss Mary in a commanding voice. Miss Manson left, followed closely by Miss Cassandra, and Freddie turned to face Miss Mary.

"That will be the last of such undisciplined behavior," said Miss Mary. "Come with me and I will show you where you are to sleep." She led the way back into the hall. "Pick up your trunks and follow me."

Freddie looked despairingly at her two heavy trunks. She picked up one in her arms and said, "I will need to return for the other one later. Perhaps one of the servants . . ."

"The pupils are the servants," said Miss Mary. "You are to be trained in housewifery along with the other more genteel arts. It is not necessary to engage servants. Mortification is good for the soul. We have one maid and one cook and two gardeners. That is sufficient for our needs."

Mutinously folding her soft mouth into a hard line, Freddie went up the stairs after Miss Mary, staggering slightly under the weight of the leather and brassbound trunk.

"Where are the other girls?" she gasped to Miss Mary's back.

"They are out on the moors, taking their botany lessons."

At last Miss Mary gained the top of the house. Doors stood ajar, revealing three dormitory-type rooms with four hard iron bedsteads in each room.

"Put your trunks over by the window," said Miss Mary. "The bed by the window will be yours. We do not have wardrobes, so you must keep your clothes in your luggage. There is one drawer in that chest over there in which each girl keeps her personal items. Breakfast is at six in the morning and dinner at two. Supper is served at six in the evening, and you are expected to be in bed by eight.

"This is a special establishment, as you no doubt know, for wayward girls who have proved themselves to be undisciplined and beyond their family's control. After two years we hope to return you to Berham Court, sufficiently meek and submissive and ready to take your place in society. We have not failed yet. Discipline is exacted for the slightest offense. Now you may go and retrieve your other trunk. And then you are not to leave this room until the bell sounds for dinner."

Freddie was too stunned by this description of the function of the seminary to do more than look at Miss Mary in blank horror.

"You have a decidedly unfortunate color of hair," added Miss Mary, surveying Freddie's flaming curls as she removed her bonnet. "Caps will be worn at all times."

"I . . . I do not have any," gasped Freddie.

"Then you must make some. Muslin will be supplied to you."

Miss Mary rustled out, and Freddie sank slowly down on the bed and stared wildly about her.

The room was deathly cold. The other three beds were tightly covered with thin blankets. The floor was sanded and scrubbed, and marks of damp had left strange patterns of faces on the lumpy whitewashed walls.

Did the earl know what this seminary was like? wondered Freddie. He must have, for he had received a letter and brochure. It was a cruel and heartless thing to do. She was to be shut away here forever among these other unwanted girls.

At last she went slowly down through the shadowy house and collected her other trunk. Panting and gasping, she managed to carry it upstairs.

All her love and admiration for the earl began to wither and die. He had sent her away like an unwanted parcel. It was now perfectly easy to understand why he was attracted by Lady

Rennenord. They were two of a kind.

A shadow fell across the room, and Freddie looked up. Miss Cassandra stood there watching her, a smile on her full lips. "Have you any money, Miss Armstrong?" she asked.

Freddie looked startled. "Lord Berham gave a package to one of the grooms to deliver to you. I assume . . ."

"Oh, *that* money," said Miss Cassandra, pouting. "A devil of a job I had getting it, too. That Manson woman was out arguing with Lord Berham's servants and saying as how they were not to pay. So I says, says I, 'You've no right for to go against your master's instructions, and you can give me that money and then be off with you and take this harridan with you.' *That's* what I said." Freddie recoiled slightly at the vulgarity of Miss Cassandra's speech. "But," went on that lady eagerly, "I mean, have you any *personal* money? I always takes charge of that, you know. Safer to leave it with me."

Freddie thought quickly about a certain twenty guineas Miss Manson had given her in the carriage with a note from Lord Berham, saying it was to buy ribbons and things, and he would send more. Conscience money, thought Freddie bitterly.

"No. I have no personal money," she lied. "Lord Berham understood that everything would be supplied her. He is going to forward me some. When it arrives, I shall let you know."

Freddie looked gloomily out of the barred

window to the great bleak expanse of the sea. "There does not seem to be much opportunity for spending anything here. Unless, of course, when we visit the shops in the town."

"Oh, you're not allowed to do that!" said Miss Cassandra. "We never go into the town. You wicked girls must be kept away from the world until you repent."

"I have nothing *to* repent," said Freddie hotly.

"But you *have*. Masquerading as a boy. Fighting in cockpits! Shameful!"

"My Lord Berham seems to have given you my life story," said Freddie bitterly, fighting back the tears which were pricking against her eyelids.

The details of Freddie's exploits had in fact come from Lady Rennenord. But Miss Cassandra knew that she was not supposed to let Freddie know that, not if she and her sister were to collect the generous bonus Lady Rennenord had promised them should they succeed in keeping the girl away from Berham Court.

"I do not understand how he could be so cruel and unfeeling," said Freddie half to herself. "I shall demand an explanation when I return at Easter."

"But you will not be returning at Easter or on any other holiday. 'Keep her with you for the holidays.' Those were Lord Berham's instructions."

Freddie sat very still on the edge of the hard bed and felt the last glimmer of hope dwindle and die. But still she made a desperate last stand. "I cannot believe Lord Berham would tell me that I was expected back at Easter and then tell you otherwise."

"Oh, you may see the letter," said Miss Cassandra, her pale eyes noticing that this offer had the effect of making Freddie's face go white and pinched. There was no such letter. Only the one from Lady Rennenord.

"Are you quite sure you have no money?" went on Miss Cassandra, running the tip of her tongue over her lips, her eyes darting at the trunks. "We must search your belongings, you know, to make sure you ain't brought anything you shouldn't."

Freddie opened her mouth to protest, but at that moment there was the faint sound of voices from downstairs.

"I'll be back," said Miss Cassandra, waddling away.

Freddie leapt into action as soon as she had gone.

She tore open the lid of one of the trunks and rummaged around until she had extracted a full suit of men's clothes and a long cloak and her sword. She raised the mattress and carefully put everything underneath. Then she quickly tucked the blankets firmly back into place. She opened her reticule and took out the bag of guineas and looked wildly about. She knew all at once that she dare not hide it anywhere in the room. She was sure that Miss Cassandra was expert at finding hiding places.

She went out onto the landing. The sound of voices came nearer. There was a carved acorn ornamenting the wooden banister at the top of the stairs. Freddie remembered hiding treasures when she was small inside the carved ornamental ball on top of the banister at home. She gave the acorn a frantic wrench and smiled as it slowly turned. She twisted it off, noticing with satisfaction that it obviously had not been used before as a hiding place. Then she popped the bag of guineas into the cavity, screwed the acorn back on, and darted back into the room to sit primly down on the edge of her bed. Just in time.

Three young ladies walked into the room.

They were pinched with cold and shabbily dressed. All three stopped short and stared at Freddie. Then one of them shrugged and walked forward. "I wish you hadn't come," she said in a voice choked with the cold. "Now we can't have the spare blankets from your bed. What have you been sent here for? Stealing the silver?"

"No," snapped Freddie.

"Oh, you'll tell us sooner or later. I'm Betty Blackstone, the one with the long nose is Freda Cartwright-Browne, and the one with the yellow hair is Jane Haddington. My sinful crime was to fall in love with the first footman. I keep writing home begging them to take me back, but they've become used to living without me. Freda ran away from home and was caught by the watch. Jane is the most exciting one. She set her family home on fire, or at least that's what they said."

"It's like a prison," gasped Freddie. "Sent to prison without a trial."

"You'll get used to it," said Betty Blackstone. "We all do. And you'll never be allowed to wear such fine clothes. They'll disappear in a day or two and be replaced with shabby duds like these we are wearing."

"But your families must visit you . . . must care."

"If anyone cares about you," said the one called Freda dryly, "then you wouldn't be sent here in the first place."

"But you're all quite *old*," said Freddie, bewildered. "This is a school. I mean, you are all as old as I. A school is for children."

"Oh, this is an excuse of a school to keep unwanted young ladies away from their families," said Jane Haddington. "It's only been here for three years, or some of us would be as old as Methuselah. I've been here the longest. I've seen three girls die since I've been here," she said with a sort of distorted pride. "Pneumonia, influenza, and malnutrition. I like funerals. We get extra food."

"But how can such a place be allowed to exist?"

Betty shrugged her thin shoulders. "Who would care? People are locked up in madhouses the whole time although they are perfectly sane, and simply because their relatives want their money, and no one does anything about *that*."

"Have you never thought of escaping?" asked Freddie.

"Some of us have tried. But you can't get very far. There's two so-called gardeners always on the lookout for stray females.

"And then, we can't get very far without any money. The townspeople think we are worse than criminals, so any girl seen in the town is promptly taken before the watch and returned here."

"But I was told I would be educated to become a young lady so that I could take my place in society," said Freddie, her eyes filling with tears.

The three young women flung themselves down on their beds and rocked with mirth.

"You *are* funny." Betty laughed. "We don't get any education at all. We do the housework, and clean, and scrub, and sew. If you can find a decent book to read, you're lucky. The only thing we don't do is cook. They're frightened we might steal the food. Our botany lesson is simply a ten-mile march supervised by one of the gardeners. There are no teachers, only the Misses Hope."

"I shall escape somehow," said Freddie, lifting her chin.

"Don't tell anyone else," said Jane Haddington. "*We're* all right, but I don't know about the other girls. You see, if you tell on someone, Miss Cassandra gives you extra food."

"How many girls are there altogether?" asked Freddie.

"Twelve altogether, including you," said Betty. "Oh, there's the dinner bell."

Dinner was served in a dingy and dark dining room. The meal consisted of two pieces of bread and a disgusting watery stew. Freddie ate her bread but passed her plate of stew to Betty. There was no talking allowed during meals, so she sat, turning over in her mind how to escape and what to do when she did.

Her grandfather's old home rightly belonged to her. But her old home, her fortune, and she herself had been left in the care of the earl until she was twenty-one. Freddie would be nineteen in June. By the time I leave here, she thought bitterly, *if* I stay, I shall be too broken in spirit to enjoy my fortune. A sudden dark thought assailed her. Perhaps the idea was that she would *never* leave alive, in which case her lands and fortune would belong to the earl!

From being that of a handsome, elegant, and dynamic man, the earl's picture changed in her mind to that of a cold-blooded aristocrat, devoid of feeling.

But still Freddie longed to see him again, if only just to give Lord Berham a piece of her mind!

Three days later Lord Berham walked restlessly up and down, wondering what to do.

His servants had returned from Lamstowe and told him a disturbing story of the vulgar fat woman who had ranted at them and insulted

Miss Manson. They reported that the seminary had looked more like a prison.

He was now debating whether to go to Lamstowe himself, when to his delight and surprise Lady Rennenord and Mrs. Bellisle were announced.

He took Lady Rennenord's hands in his, studying with pleasure her calm and beautiful face, her exquisite figure, and the thick, glossy curls peeping out from beneath a delicious confection of a bonnet.

"Welcome back," he said. "I had not expected the pleasure of your company so soon. Pray be seated, ladies, and let me offer you a dish of tea. Did you enjoy your visit?"

"Very much," barked Mrs. Bellisle. "Got rid of that girl, did you?"

"Miss Armstrong left us five days ago." The earl frowned and studied the shining toecaps of his boots. "I confess I am a trifle worried about this seminary. I am sure you would not have recommended anywhere unsuitable, Lady Rennenord. Have you actually seen this establishment yourself?"

"No, Lord Berham. But it is highly recommended. Of course, Miss Armstrong has no doubt sent a letter by your servants, complaining bitterly. She is very young and needs to learn."

"It is not that," said the earl, becoming more worried by the minute. "My servants tell me that one of the principals is a fat, vulgar woman

85

who berated and insulted poor Miss Manson and sent her packing as soon as Miss Armstrong had arrived."

"Servants' gossip," sniffed Mrs. Bellisle. "That sort of low person is always dramatizing things."

"My servants are very trustworthy and reliable," said Lord Berham coldly. "Admittedly, they are all very, very fond of Miss Armstrong. Oh, my *dear* Lady Rennenord! You must not distress yourself."

For Lady Rennenord's beautiful eyes had filled with tears. "I was genuinely trying to do the best for the girl," she said, allowing two large tears to roll unchecked down her cheeks. "Perhaps I should not have said anything. You were so worried about her, my lord, that my heart was moved. If you will forgive my saying so, my lord, I fear Miss Armstrong has really not been brought up to consider the comfort or welfare of anyone other than herself. Naturally, she does not want to leave a grand mansion to go back to school! It is humiliating. But *necessary*, my lord. How could she make her debut as she is at present when she might challenge someone at Almack's to a duel?"

"I am sure you are right," said the earl, "although she is far from being selfish. She was extremely concerned about all my servants' welfare and seemed to know all their ailments," he added with a reminiscent smile.

"Well," said Lady Rennenord, delicately drying her eyes, "that is all very commendable, although a trifle lacking in breeding. It is a mistake to be too familiar with the lower orders. They take advantage."

She saw the earl frown again and added quickly, "I will go myself this very day to Lamstowe to see the dear girl and so will put your fears at rest."

"That is very generous," said the earl warmly, "and so like you. But all this is not at all necessary. We are forgetting Miss Manson! *She* is an educated and sensible woman and will give us a good account of what actually happened."

For a moment Lady Rennenord seemed to be in the grip of some strong emotion. Poor, pretty thing, thought the earl indulgently. She really fears she has displeased me.

"Let us forget about Miss Armstrong," he said. "Tell me about your visit, and I will try *not* to tell you a hundred times how very much I have missed you."

The visit passed pleasantly.

Lady Rennenord and Mrs. Bellisle were no sooner seated in their carriage and leaving Berham Court than Lady Rennenord asked suddenly, "This Manson woman. Who owns that cottage of hers?"

"I do," said Mrs. Bellisle promptly.

"And does she always pay her rent?"

"Always," said Mrs. Bellisle. "That's what I like about her. No fuss. No endless demands for repairs. She's got a little money that was left her by some relative. Not much, but it seems sufficient for her needs. I only charge her a token sum."

"I think I had better pay her a call," said Lady Rennenord, "if you would not mind setting me down. There is no need for you to accompany me."

"Of course, you are concerned about our dear Miss Armstrong," said Mrs. Bellisle sarcastically.

"I am concerned that Miss Manson will turn out to be one of those hysterical spinsters who will trouble Lord Berham with a great deal of nonsense," said Lady Rennenord calmly.

"And you want to get to her first," said Mrs. Bellisle with a tinge of sarcasm.

"Of course."

"Very well. But Miss Manson is not at all hysterical. I told you she was the ideal person to accompany Miss Armstrong. Very religious and strict. You will find she has not approved of Miss Armstrong's unconventionality one whit. You know her yourself, Clarissa. You have met her several times. She knows her place."

Miss Manson was weeding a flower bed in her garden as the carriage drew up. She had been rehearsing the speech she would make to Lord Berham when she called on him that afternoon. Miss Manson was determined that Miss Armstrong should be brought home, but she was shy of approaching such a great personage as Lord Berham without a great deal of rehearsal.

Besides, did she need to say anything? Did she need to complain about a seminary so highly recommended by Lady Rennenord? The whole of Berham knew that the earl was enamored of her ladyship. And Miss Armstrong would be home again at Easter, which was only a few weeks away. But Miss Manson's conscience nagged her more and more. She had grown extremely fond of the girl and could not bear to think of her living in that place under the rule of those terrible women even for a day.

She straightened her back and saw Lady Rennenord descending from Mrs. Bellisle's carriage.

Miss Manson nervously wiped her hands on her apron and dropped Lady Rennenord a low curtsy. Lady Rennenord graciously gave her two fingers to shake.

"Shall we step inside your charming cottage for a little, Miss Manson?" she said. "I am anxious to have a private chat with you."

Miss Manson pinned a servile smile on her face and curtsied again before leading the way into the cottage.

Lady Rennenord sat down in the small parlor and looked about her with calm, lipid eyes. The furniture was old but comfortable and well cared for. A copper jug of daffodils shone in the gloom of the low-raftered parlor. A bright homemade hooked rug decorated the floor. There were several quite good watercolors on the walls.

"Very comfortable," remarked Lady Rennenord, fanning herself languidly although the room was quite cold. "I gather from Mrs.

Bellisle that you pay quite a modest rent."

"Yes, my lady. Mrs. Bellisle is most generous. She takes, as you know, a great interest in the welfare of the indigent gentlewomen of Berham and was pleased to offer me the tenancy of this cottage when the seminary closed. May I offer your ladyship some refreshment?"

"I thank you, no. It has often been pointed out to Mrs. Bellisle that she could charge a much higher rent for this cottage. You must be very grateful to her. She is not famous for her generosity. You will forgive me for speaking plain."

Miss Manson felt her heart sink. She knew very well the reason for all these remarks about her rent. The clutch-fisted Mrs. Bellisle charged Miss Manson a low rent simply because she occasionally liked to appear generous, and Miss Manson knew how to creep and toady to a nicety, having learned in the hard school of impoverished gentility. If you were of the wrong sex — female — and the wrong class — gentry — and you had barely enough to eat, then like the Miss Mansons of the world, you learned quickly how to flatter and manipulate and stoop to all sorts of disgraceful subterfuges to keep yourself from the workhouse.

What Lady Rennenord was actually saying was that if Miss Manson dared to complain to Lord Berham about the seminary in Lamstowe, Lady Rennenord would use all her influence to see that Manson's rent was increased drastically or that Miss Manson was put out of her cottage.

Miss Manson understood all this very well.

"I am very grateful to Mrs. Bellisle," said Miss Manson, "and to you, my lady, for having put me in the way of my recent, if short, employment."

"Ah, yes, escorting Miss Armstrong. Lord Berham is overconcerned in that direction. His servants came to him with some wild tale of insults and abuse."

"Well, that was indeed the —"

"But you are a sensible women, Miss Manson, and I know you will not dream of upsetting Lord Berham by encouraging such stupid gossip. Mrs. Bellisle and myself have Lord Berham's happiness very much at heart, and I trust you will not say anything that would add to our . . . I mean, of course, *his* anxiety."

Miss Manson was overcome with a sudden and savage desire to slap Lady Rennenord's face. But she lowered her eyes and said meekly, "I would not dream of distressing his lordship."

"See that you don't," said Lady Rennenord, shutting her fan with a snap.

After she had left, Miss Manson cried long and bitterly. Shakespeare had been wrong. It was not conscience that made cowards of us all, but lack of money.

The sound of another carriage arriving made her dry her eyes quickly. This would undoubtedly be Lord Berham.

His tall figure seemed to fill the little parlor. He began without preamble.

"I have heard a distressing tale from my servants of your visit to the seminary in Lamstowe," he began, his black eyes resting on Miss Manson's averted face. "They say that one of the Misses Hope was a coarse, fat woman who abused you most shamefully."

"Indeed, my lord?"

"You don't think so?"

"There was a certain altercation," said Miss Manson in a low voice, "but nothing to become exercised over."

"And did Miss Armstrong seem as if she would be happy there?"

"She was . . . was naturally much distressed. We had become close friends. It is understandable. One does not think of putting a female of eighteen years of age in a seminary."

"But I was given to understand it was more of a school for deportment."

"Yes, my lord, you could call it that."

There was a short silence. Then the earl said, "Are you very sure that Miss Armstrong will be happy there?"

"This is a very pleasant cottage, don't you think, my lord?" said Miss Manson, apparently inconsequentially.

"Yes," said the earl, surprised. "It is. But I beg you to answer my question."

Miss Manson took a deep breath. "Miss Armstrong will be returning for the Easter holidays, my lord. It is a short time away. I think you can safely leave matters until then. If Miss

Armstrong is unhappy, she will tell you. Of that I am sure."

"Very well," said the earl, giving her a somewhat puzzled look. "We will wait until then. And now here is payment for you services, Miss Manson." He placed a wallet on the table.

"Thank you," she whispered, tears starting to her eyes.

He looked at her curiously, waiting to see if she would say anything further, but she merely stood before him with her head bowed.

He left, feeling uneasy.

A letter which arrived from Freddie a week later should have been comforting, but the earl could only puzzle and wonder over it. First of all, the handwriting was small and crabbed and did not seem to belong to someone with Freddie's generous spirit. Although her grandfather's lawyers had implied that Freddie's schooling had not been of the best and that an entry to Oxford University would require an enrollment in a crammer first, the earl had not thought that the girl's grammar or spelling would be quite so bad.

The letter read:

My dear Lord Berham, Things is Very Nice here what with the wether becoming more mild. Do not send for me at Eester since I am Very Happy to stay with my beluvd Misses Hope who are that kind to me it would bring Tears to your Eyes could you see it. Please send money. Always your faithful and obeddent ward, Frederica.

But then, ladies were never famous for their spelling or grammar, as the earl very well knew, having been the recipient of many love letters.

He resolved to send her money and tell her that he would nonetheless visit her at Easter. Then he took Lady Rennenord out driving in his curricle. She fascinated him more and more each day. Her calm face and eyes seemed to belie the ripe promise of her figure. Her caressing ways and delicate movements, which all seemed every day to reveal a new charm of her body to his eyes, almost made him forget the worry about his ward. He had meant to mention Freddie's strange letter to Lady Rennenord but did not want to break the magic spell of their outing.

Lady Rennenord always seemed distressed when he mentioned Freddie's name, and he felt sure it was because she was as worried over the choice of seminary as he was.

That evening he called on Miss Manson again, but the cottage was locked and barred. Neighbors told him that Miss Manson had said she was going on a short visit to relatives. So that was that.

He was sure that he was worrying about nothing. Freddie was probably laughing and joking with her new friends, without a care in the world.

At that moment Freddie was locked down in the coal cellar of the seminary. She had been there all day.

She had thought long and hard over the earl's thoughtless treatment of her and finally had come to the conclusion that there must have been some mistake.

And so she had gone to the study of the Misses Hope directly after breakfast and demanded to see his letter. Miss Mary had railed at her for her insolence and, seizing the birch rod from the corner, had proceeded to lash Freddie. Freddie had finally wrested the rod from her, broken it over her knee, and thrown the pieces in Miss Mary's face. The "gardeners," or wardens, as Freddie thought of them, had come rushing in to the study in answer to Miss Mary's screams, and Freddie had been thrown down into the coal cellar.

She was wretched with cold and hunger. She began to wonder if they meant to starve her to death. All the long day Freddie had been searching for a way out. There was a small glassless window up at ground level, but it was barred.

She looked miserably at the coal and wondered if it would be possible to eat it. The only thing to cheer her imprisonment had been the discovery of a candle and a lucifer. At least she could have some light. But she hesitated to light the candle so soon. It would have to last the night.

How she wished she had tried to escape instead of feeling so crushed and defeated by Lord Berham's seeming indifference to her fate!

The cellar grew blacker. Freddie lit the candle and tried not to think of rats.

There was a rustling in the undergrowth outside. No doubt some nocturnal animal, thought Freddie, free to roam and prowl.

A faint voice whispered, "Frederica."

Freddie stiffened and then sighed. It was the wind in the trees. Nothing more.

"I hope I am not going mad with hunger," she said worriedly.

And then it came again. "Frederica!"

"I'm here!" cried Freddie urgently, hoping she was not calling out to a figment of her imagination.

A face suddenly appeared at the small, barred window. Freddie seized the candle and held it up.

A gypsy woman with her head tied up in a ragged scarlet scarf, her swarthy face looking evil in the flickering light, stared back. Freddie nearly dropped the candle in her fright.

"Don't you recognize me?" said the gypsy woman plaintively. "It is I, Miss Manson."

"Miss *Manson!*" shrieked Freddie. "How . . ."

"Shhhh!" said Miss Manson urgently. "They'll hear us."

Freddie looked about and saw a box, which she carried under the window to stand upon. Miss Manson was lying on the ground outside, her face on a level with the barred window.

"Lord Berham gave me money for escorting you," she whispered, "so I decided to take the mail coach and come and see you. I called here yesterday, but I could not think how I was to see you without letting the Hope women see *me*. For they would write to Lady Rennenord, and I would lose my cottage."

She saw the puzzled expression on Freddie's face and added hurriedly, "Never mind that now. Today I was out on the moor dressed like this. It is a good disguise, is it not? People are frightened of gypsies and do not like to come too close.

"I saw the girls being marched across the moor for their exercise by one of the menservants. I sat by the side of the path. They all walked past me, averting their eyes, but one of the ones at the end stumbled. She had fair hair and a very red nose."

"Jane Haddington," whispered Freddie. "Go on."

"I muttered to her low, 'Where is Frederica?' and she said, 'In the coal cellar, locked up.' Then the manservant started shouting at her, and she ran to join the others. He asked her if I had said anything, and — Jane, is it? — said, to my relief, 'She just wanted to tell my fortune.' I waited until now and, well, here I am."

"Oh, Miss Manson," said Freddie urgently, "you cannot know how grateful I am to see you. This is a truly dreadful place. Does Lord

Berham know how very dreadful it is?"

"I will tell you all about that once you are released," whispered Miss Manson. "How thin and white you are! I brought you some food and wine. You must eat it quickly and drink the wine and hand me back the bottle."

Freddie's eyes glistened as a large pasty was edged sideways through the bars, followed by a bottle of wine.

"Gently with the wine," urged Miss Manson, "or you will spill it. I have taken out the cork."

She waited anxiously while Freddie fell on the food and drank the whole bottle of wine.

"I was so thirsty," Freddie explained, grinning drunkenly. "At least I shall sleep like the dead."

"Do you think they will let you out tonight?"

"No," said Freddie. "Perhaps tomorrow. I shall be truly servile and humble and repentant, and then, once I am out, I shall fetch my boy's clothes from under my mattress and meet you tomorrow when they are all asleep."

"The house is all locked and barred," said Miss Manson urgently. "How will you escape?"

"Somehow," said Freddie. "I will meet you outside the gates at midnight. Go now, before they find you."

As the evening shadows lengthened on the next day, Freddie began to lose hope. Maybe they really *did* want her to starve to death. She was dreadfully hungry, and the wine of the night before had given her a raging thirst.

But just before supper the door was unlocked. Freddie was dragged out by one of the menservants, and then she was paraded in front of the other girls as an example of what would happen to any girl who dared to be insolent.

She looked a pathetic and dirty sight, covered as she was with coal dust.

But she was allowed bread and water for supper and was sent to her room before the other girls, which suited Freddie very well. She carefully removed her bag of guineas from its hiding place and put them under her pillow. Then she undressed, got into bed, and turned her face to the wall. She pretended to be asleep when the other girls returned.

She stayed like that while the other girls undressed, talking in low whispers about "poor Frederica" and Jane told about the strange gypsy woman who had asked for her.

Freddie lay waiting until at last she was sure that all the girls were asleep. She cursed herself for having made the arrangement to meet Miss Manson at midnight. How on earth could she, Freddie, tell when midnight was?

She quietly drew out her suit of clothes, first putting on her chest binder of linen and buckram. Then she wrapped herself in her cloak and fastened her sword at her side. Next she tied the bag of guineas onto her belt.

She took a last look at the sleeping figures of the other girls, feeling a pang of pity. She had not become close friends with any of them, since the girls were like prisoners, grumbling about the same things day in and day out in a sort of hopeless monotone.

Freddie felt her way down the stairs to the hall, her heart leaping into her mouth every time a board creaked.

She hesitated in the hall. At the back of the hall, the study door stood invitingly open, revealed by the thin shafts of moonlight striking through the tall narrow panes of glass on either side of the front door.

Freddie was overcome by a burning desire to see the correspondence about her. She crept into the study. The remains of a fire glowed on the hearth. Freddie lit a candle and then approached the large mahogany desk in the corner. She began to search through the drawers. Nothing here but old receipts and household accounts. One large drawer at the bottom was locked.

Freddie picked up the poker from the hearth, wedged it into the drawer, and snapped the lock, waiting and listening while the crack of splintering wood seemed to reverberate through the house. For some time all she could hear was the pounding of her own heart. No one called out.

Freddie gently slid out the drawer. There were twelve files, each marked with a girl's name. It was then that Freddie saw an old carpetbag in the corner, and the glimmerings of an idea came to her. She quickly stuffed all the files into the bag and then silently left the study.

The front door had to be tackled. All its many bolts and chains had to be dealt with slowly, one at a time, until at last the door stood open.

The weedy drive to freedom stretched out in front of her in the moonlight.

The gates at the end of the drive were locked, but Freddie quickly scaled them, negotiating the spikes at the top with ease. She dropped down on the other side, holding the carpetbag and looking about eagerly.

Miss Manson, dressed in her normal clothes, quickly detached herself from the shadow of the wall.

Freddie put a finger to her lips, and together both women began to hurry along the cliff path and then down into the town of Lamstowe.

Chapter 5

The earl sat at his ease in Mrs. Bellisle's garden, admiring the turn of Lady Rennenord's wrist as she poured tea into thin china cups.

Sun and shadow dappled her face. A light spring breeze lazily moved the thin folds of her muslin gown and set the fringes of her stole dancing.

The earl felt remarkably at peace with the world. No more odd letters had arrived from Lamstowe. He planned to propose marriage to Lady Rennenord and at the same time suggest removing Frederica from the seminary and giving her a Season in London.

The arrival of Lady Rennenord's brother, Harry Struthers-Benton, had marred the earl's sylvan idyll slightly. He was all the earl detested in a man. He usually dressed in what he considered the ultra-pitch of fashion, collared like the leader of a four-horse team, pinched in the middle like an hourglass, and wearing cravats as ample as tablecloths.

He larded his conversation with names of the rich and famous.

He had fair hair back-combed until it stood up like the feathers of a Friesland hen. Like his sister, he was quite stupid, but unlike her, he had not learned to conceal the fact.

He was mercifully absent on that sunny day, and the earl was finally beginning to think he had put off proposing to Lady Rennenord long enough.

What saved Lady Rennenord from making the same social mistakes as her brother was a sort of shrewdness which in a peasant would be referred to as native cunning. She was as narcissistic as her brother, but she had a good dress sense and practiced for hours in front of the long glass in her bedroom until she had every seductive movement perfected. The earl did not know that when she bent down to tie the satin ribbon of her slipper, thereby causing the thin muslin of her gown to strain against her breasts, it was a movement that had been as well rehearsed as any speech by Mrs. Siddons.

If Lady Rennenord had been a clever woman, she would have let Freddie stay, for the nature of the seminary to which Freddie had been sent was bound to come out sooner or later. But Lady Rennenord planned to be married to the earl by then, and marriage, to her, was an end in itself. Her late husband had been a bluff, handsome man who had never quite got over finding out that the pretty, delicate girl he had married was a coldhearted shrew who did not care a rap for him. From being in love with her, he became equally afraid of her and her malicious tongue, and so she was allowed to do as she pleased. Lady Rennenord fully believed she could handle the earl in the same way.

"Where is Mrs. Bellisle?" asked the earl.

"She is gone to make calls in the town."

"And your brother?"

"Harry has gone to attend to some business." Harry had been all but forcibly ejected from the house ten minutes before the earl's arrival.

"Good." The earl smiled. "There is something I have to say to you, Clarissa. Something of great importance."

A warm tide of victory swept over Clarissa Rennenord. This was it!

She unfurled a lace parasol, leaned back in her chair, and smiled sweetly on the earl. "Yes, my lord?" she murmured.

"I . . ." began the earl, and then stopped.

The sound of a horse being ridden hard up the drive came to their ears. Then there was a tremendous pounding at the front door, which was on the other side of the house from where they were sitting.

"Go on, Lord Berham," said Lady Rennenord urgently.

The sounds of a loud altercation came to their ears. "I think perhaps we had better find out who is disturbing the peace," said the earl.

Mrs. Bellisle's butler came walking towards them, his face flushed.

"My lady," he said, "a certain individual has

called. He will not go until he has spoken to you personally. He says after you have seen this letter, you will have a reply for him."

Lady Rennenord took the letter and smiled apologetically at the earl. "If you will forgive me, my lord. This will not take long. I cannot think . . ."

She broke off and stared down at the letter she had opened. Miss Cassandra Hope's semi-literate scrawl seemed to leap off the page:

Dear Lady Rennenord, We are in Such distress that hell-cat Frederica having escaped and taken all the letters from us and gone the Lord knows where. She must not reach Lord Berham for raisins that are obvious. Tell him she stole the Silver which is what we have told the majestrate at Lamstowe. My sister has the palpitashuns Bad. Your servent, Cassandra Hope."

"Bad news?" said the earl with quick concern, noticing that the color had drained completely from his fair companion's face.

"Oh, 'tis nothing," said her ladyship with a shrill laugh. "I shall speak to this fellow. Pray do not leave."

Lady Rennenord hurried into the house. The servant from the seminary was waiting in the hall. "I shall give you my reply directly," said Lady Rennenord.

She went into the drawing room, sat down at a

writing desk, and drew a sheet of paper towards herself. The door opened, and her brother ambled in. Lady Rennenord swung round. "I told you to keep out of the way, Harry," she snapped. "Lord Berham was about to propose, and *this* arrived." She held out Cassandra's letter with a shaking hand.

Harry put up his glass and studied the letter. "Who's Frederica?" he asked.

"Oh, of course you don't know," said his sister. Quickly she outlined the details of Freddie's masquerade and the plot to keep her in the seminary until she, Lady Rennenord, became the countess of Berham. "What am I to do?" wailed Lady Rennenord. "She may already be on her way to Berham with that letter I wrote."

"She's probably dressed as a boy, since they ain't been able to find her," said Harry. "I ran into Cramble t'other day. Send him with two fellows to smoke her out. He knows what she looks like. They'll get rid of her."

Clarissa Rennenord looked at her brother in dawning admiration. "I did not know you could be so clever, Harry."

"Well, there you are. Don't worry. Cramble'll hunt her down, never fear."

"What if she should reach Berham before Cramble finds her?"

"Has she any money?"

"No. They always take any money away from the girls. Mrs. Haddington — you remember her — told me all about the place."

"Then she'll have to walk. She daren't go to the authorities, and if she does, they'll just hand her back. Probably starving to death in some ditch by now."

"Let me write a reply to Cassandra Hope. Make yourself scarce, Harry. Berham has *got* to propose before he leaves here this day."

But when Clarissa Rennenord returned to the garden, the earl was already on his feet and showing all the signs of a gentleman about to take his leave.

"Well, that's finished with," said Lady Rennenord gaily. "Do sit down. You were about to ask me something?"

But the moment had passed. Clouds had covered the sun, and the day had grown cold. Lord Berham's mood also had changed in temperature. Somehow he did not want to commit himself yet.

"It was nothing of importance," said the earl easily.

"But I am sure it was," said Clarissa Rennenord with a certain edge to her voice which made the earl look down at her in surprise.

"It can't have been very important," he said, picking up his hat and cane, "for I have quite forgotten what it was I was about to say."

She turned her head away and bit her lip, the movement showing the perfection of her bosom and the white column of her neck.

The earl hesitated.

"Hullo! Hullo!" said a cheerful voice. "Not

interrupting anything, am I?"

Harry came strolling across the lawn. "You two got anything to tell me?" he went on, looking arch.

"No. Nothing at all." The earl bent over Lady Rennenord's hand, which trembled slightly in his grasp.

He made his good-byes, walked away round the front of the house, and climbed into his curricle.

When he arrived home, he picked up the letters which had arrived while he was out and walked into the library, turning them over.

There was one dingy and dirty one which caught his attention. The one shilling and one penny postage, which had been paid by his butler, showed that the letter had come from some distance. He broke the seal.

Dear Lord Berham, I have run away from the seminary because they starved and beat me. I am in hiding because the mail coaches and stagecoaches are being watched, since Miss Mary Hope has told the authorities that I stole the silver, which is a Lie.

I shall try to reach Berham by walking across country as soon as I think it is safe to venture forth. Your Loving Ward, Frederica Armstrong.

Lord Berham put down the letter. Then he picked it up again and read it carefully. He rummaged in his desk until he found the other letter which was supposed to have come from Freddie and compared them.

At last he shook his head in vexation. There was only one possible course of action. He must ride to Lamstowe himself.

It had taken Frederica and Miss Manson two days to travel there, because he had arranged for them to journey by easy stages. If he took his best team harnessed to his racing curricle, he could be confident of reaching Lamstowe some time before dawn.

If Freddie and Miss Manson had been more alert on all suits, they would have hired a carriage the night of Freddie's escape and journeyed to meet the mail coach. That way they could have been nearly back at Berham before the alert was sounded.

But Miss Manson had some of the money that Lord Berham had given her, which amounted to ten pounds, and Freddie had her twenty guineas, and so they felt very rich. With Freddie dressed as a boy and no one knowing of Miss Manson's presence, they were confident of passing unnoticed in Lamstowe. Both were quite giddy with triumph over Freddie's escape. All Freddie could think of was lots and lots of food followed by a bath and hours and hours of sleep.

Miss Manson had already bespoken rooms for them at an inn in Lamstowe, telling the landlord that her "nephew" would be joining her and that they would require a very late supper, perhaps as late as one in the morning.

Since the inn served all the local fishermen, it was busy most of the night as well as the day. Lights were blazing in a welcome way when Freddie and Miss Manson arrived.

Freddie ate until she thought she would burst, paid grandly for the maids to fill up a tin bath with hot water, and then fell into a soundless sleep, not waking until the sun was high in the sky the next day.

Miss Manson had awakened earlier, but not very much earlier. She decided to go out and take a walk and see whether Freddie's escape had occasioned any interest in the town.

She had only gone a few steps from the inn when she found that it had caused a full-scale hunt. She stopped beside the group of townspeople and asked them what the matter was, why there were men searching every house.

A terrible monster of a girl had escaped from that seminary up on the cliffs, they said. She had nearly murdered one of the principals and had made off with the silver. It would be a hanging matter when they got her.

Miss Manson felt a cold hand clutch her heart. She drew back into the shadow of the inn courtyard as she recognized the squat figure of Miss Cassandra Hope coming along the street with the two menservants from the seminary.

"She didn't take none of her clothes," she

heard Miss Cassandra say as she passed. "Stands to reason she might be dressed as a boy. Though where she could have hid the clothes, I'm blessed if I know."

Miss Manson ran back to the inn and erupted into Freddie's room, babbling out the terrible news.

"I never thought of taking one dress," groaned Freddie. "They took away all the clothes I brought from Berham and replaced them with two shabby gowns. I was *glad* to leave them. *Now* what am I to do?"

There was a commotion in the inn yard, and Miss Manson opened the window and looked down. The two menservants had just entered the inn yard and were questioning the landlord.

"Back into bed," cried Miss Manson. "Quickly!"

She rummaged in her reticule, murmuring, "It is as well I am such a vain lady, for I never travel without my paint."

"What are you *doing?*" cried Freddie as Miss Manson began to tumble pots of cosmetics over the coverlet.

"Shhh!" said that lady, "and let me work."

Five minutes later there came a pounding at the door. Miss Manson opened it and stood barring the way, looking every inch the respectable spinster. The menservants from the seminary had not seen her before, and luckily Miss Cassandra was not with them.

"We're looking for one of the young ladies

that escaped from the seminary," growled one. "Landlord's given us permission to search the rooms."

"There is only my nephew and me," replied Miss Manson. "He is very ill, and I do not wish him disturbed."

"Oh, well, in that case." The man made to turn away, but his companion muttered something to him. They both faced Miss Manson.

"Well, madam," said one gruffly, "if you'll just stand aside and let us have a look at your nephew."

"Of course I will not!" snapped Miss Manson. "It is a girl you seek."

"A girl who might be dressed as a boy," replied one of the men, grinning. "Stand aside or we'll come back with the parish constable."

Miss Manson stood reluctantly aside. The two men strode into the room and stood looking down at the figure in the bed. Freddie's bright hair had been tied up in a linen bandage. Her face was chalk-white and covered with angry-looking red spots.

The men began to back away from the bed.

"What's the matter with him?" growled one.

"I do not know," said Miss Manson, fluttering her hands helplessly. "I am awaiting the physician. Let us hope and pray it is *not* the smallpox. I told the boy's mother to have him immunized, but she would not listen."

But Miss Manson said her last words to the empty air. The two men had fled after the sound of that dreaded word, "smallpox."

"Now we must leave this town," whispered Miss Manson urgently.

"I don't think so," said Freddie. "They'll be searching everywhere. After a few days, the last place they will look will be here in Lamstowe. I must alter my appearance, and so must you. I shall give you a list. There is another inn at the far end of the town. We will move there under our new personalities."

Later that day, the other inn, the Duke of Marlborough, found that it had two new guests, in the shape of Mr. Manson and his nephew. Mr. Manson was a tall, bony, finicky gentleman who walked with mincing steps and kept tripping over his sword. His nephew was a spotty, fat-faced youth with dusty black hair.

Miss Manson had bought herself a suit of gentleman's clothes, and Freddie had altered her own appearance by stuffing wax pads in her cheeks to fatten her face, leaving some of the spots painted on, and covering her red hair with a black wig. She was able to alter her slim figure with a generous amount of buckram wadding.

Both settled down to a quiet existence, going for long walks along the harbor and discussing endlessly how to get revenge on Mary and Cassandra Hope.

To Freddie's disappointment her own file stolen from the seminary contained only the letter from Lord Berham which he had sent with the money for her tuition. It baldly stated that he was consigning his ward to their care. There were no other letters, only a paper listing a note of the Misses Hopes' estimate of Freddie's unruly character and itemizing the clothes she had brought with her.

The other letters were more incriminating. Money sent by parents to their daughters had been appropriated by Cassandra, and notes made to that effect. There was also evidence that the letters the girls wrote home never left the seminary, replaced by letters written by Miss Cassandra.

Thus, Freddie, despite Miss Manson's assurances to the contrary, was still in two minds about Lord Berham's character. The main stumbling block to thinking well of him was the earl's courtship of Lady Rennenord. But then, her grandfather had told her that men only wanted one thing. Perhaps that explained it.

Freddie also was much troubled by the memory of the scenes she had witnessed in the brothel. Did all women behave so? Freddie found that she could not indulge in daydreams about future lovers without those terrible pictures of the facts of life dancing before her eyes.

At last she haltingly confided her fears to Miss Manson. Now, you cannot live for years in the countryside, particularly around harvest time, and not have ample enough demonstration of the peculiar mating dance of the human race. Miss Manson, although she was shocked to the soul by Freddie's grandfather's behavior, tried to do her best to allay Freddie's fears. That sort of thing, she said repressively, was necessary after marriage, though not in the raw, lewd state that Freddie had witnessed. Ladies *never* enjoyed that sort of thing, said Miss Manson wisely. The only women who did belonged to the Fashionable Impure. It was the cross womanhood had to bear in order to enter the security of a marriage and have children.

With that, Miss Manson dabbed the perspiration from her brow and felt that for a spinster, she had acquitted herself very well and had laid all Freddie's fears to rest.

But after Miss Manson had retired for the night, Freddie slipped out of the inn and walked down to the harbor in the moonlight. She tried not to admit to herself that the handsome face and figure of Lord Berham were beginning to enter her dreams more than she could have wished. Her thoughts about him were gradually becoming upsetting, and the very idea of him made her body feel strange.

She sat for a long time on the harbor wall. The night was very still and calm. Stars danced and bobbed in the water, and far out to sea she could see the riding lights of the fishing boats. All at once Freddie decided that it surely would be safe now to go back to Berham. They could not still be watching the stagecoaches, and even if they were, she was sure that their disguises were perfect.

She wondered if Lord Berham would be glad

to see her. What if he believed the principals of the seminary's terrible accusations and turned her over to the authorities? She would hang or be deported.

Freddie sat for a very long time, remembering everything she could about Lord Berham. He surely would not keep a staff of such likable and contented servants if he were a hard and ruthless man.

Freddie was reluctant to go back into the inn. There was no one about. She was able to relax only when she could escape from people. In the daytime crowds, although she went out as little as possible, there was always the nagging fear that a voice would cry, "Stop, thief!" or that a heavy hand would fall on her shoulder.

Gradually the sky began to pale in the east. Soon the fishing boats would be coming home and the quay would be alive with men and nets and baskets full of their glittering catch.

A dawn breeze came up, blowing from the land, bringing with it the smell of wood smoke and evergreen and the damp feel of rain to come.

The pads inside her cheeks felt as if they had become larger and larger. Freddie took a quick look about. There was no one in sight. She took the pads out of her cheeks and then with one quick movement removed her wig and shook out her red curls, which had grown to a more girlish length since Berham. She placed the wig and the wax pads beside her on the harbor wall.

That is how Captain Cramble and his two ruffians hired for the search found her.

They had been drinking at the other inn, having returned to Lamstowe after diligently searching the surrounding countryside. They had become so noisy and vulgar that the landlord had ejected them, so they had gone in search of Lamstowe's other hostelry, the Duke of Marlborough.

Captain Cramble saw the slim figure with the red hair sitting in the dawn light on the harbor wall.

"There she is," he whispered excitedly. "Close in on her before she sees us, and make sure she doesn't reach for her sword."

His two companions looked at him with puzzled sneers. What was there to be frightened of? A mere girl with a toy for a sword?

But the captain had drunk too much. In his efforts to creep up on Freddie, who had her back to them and was dreamily gazing out to sea, he staggered and clutched at a pile of fishing baskets for support. The baskets gave way, and with a great oath, the captain fell on the quay.

Freddie started to her feet and swung around, pulling out her sword.

The two ruffians began to close in on her, eyeing the sword warily. But the captain, who had risen to his feet, was determined to waste no time dueling with Freddie, who, he already knew, was expert in the use of the small sword.

He prized up a cobble and threw it straight at

her. Freddie saw it coming too late. The heavy stone struck her full on the forehead, and she dropped unconscious onto the quay.

"Well, that's that," said the captain, rubbing his hands.

"What do we do with the gentry mort?" growled one of his ruffians. "Take 'er to the magistrate?"

"No," said the captain. "One look at your phiz and he'd arrest *you*. We take her off to a place I know of and hide her away for as long as possible."

One of the men bent down, picked Freddie up, and slung her light, inert body over his shoulder.

The earl of Berham's curricle, driven by a stout groom sitting beside him rolled to a halt in front of the inn.

The earl jumped down, calling on his groom to hold his team. Pulling out a pistol, he headed purposefully towards the group on the harbor. He fired a shot over their heads.

"Berham," shouted the captain. "Run for it!"

"The girl!" said the man who was holding Freddie. "What do we do with the girl?"

"Throw her in the water," snarled the captain.

The man tossed Freddie over the harbor wall, and the three men began to race off down the quay.

The earl wasted no time running after them. Stripping off his coat, he stopped only for a moment to tug off his boots. Then he leapt to the top of the harbor wall and dived down into the sea, catching Freddie's unconscious body as it slowly surfaced. He swam with her over to the steps and dragged her up onto the quay. He pumped her arms backwards and forwards until sea water gushed from her mouth and she gave a groan.

People were running from the inn, awakened by the sound of the shot.

"Oh, God! Is she dead?"

The earl looked up and found Miss Manson looking down at him, wringing her hands. She was dressed in man's clothes.

The earl stopped and picked Freddie up. "Lead the way," he said curtly to Miss Manson. "You have a great deal of explaining to do."

Some hours later, when Freddie had recovered enough to speak, the earl was in possession of most of the facts, with one notable exception. Miss Manson had not told him of Lady Rennenord's visit. For Miss Manson knew that great people might promise to stand by you, but they were apt to forget you as soon as you were out of sight. And so, fearing she would find herself without a home, Miss Manson kept silent on the subject of Lady Rennenord. But she did make the earl give his word he would not tell anyone in the town of Berham about her part in Freddie's escape. Although the earl protested that he was deeply grateful to her and chided her for not coming to him in the first place, Miss Manson was adamant. All she wanted to do, she said, was return to her cottage and forget about the whole thing.

The earl carefully studied the documents Freddie had stolen from the seminary. Then he went to fetch the parish constable, the magistrate, and the local militia. They all headed up the cliffs to the seminary, where they found the eleven girls raiding the kitchen. The Misses Hope had fled along with their servants. Somehow they had learned of the earl's arrival.

The girls, assured that their word would be believed, told the earl and the authorities their terrible tales of bullying and near starvation.

Arrangements were made for some of the local ladies to supervise their welfare until their parents arrived to take them away.

After an exhausting day, the earl returned to the inn, pushing his way into the yard through a thick crowd of sightseers. The news about the seminary had spread like wildfire, and Freddie was the heroine of the day, although her exploits were vastly exaggerated. That she had fought off three men with her bare hands and had chased the wicked sisters from town were just two of the tales that were circulating about her.

Miss Manson, dressed in her own clothes, was sitting and reading beside Freddie's bed. Freddie was asleep, her face still looking thin and pinched. There was a great purple bruise on her forehead.

She was fast asleep.

"The physician says she will recover," said

Miss Manson softly. "He wished to bleed her, but I would not let him. She is so weak."

"What was Cramble doing in Lamstowe, think you?" asked the earl, pulling up a chair to the other side of the bed.

"Looking for Miss Armstrong, I believe," said Miss Manson. "It would be too much of a coincidence were he to be here by accident."

"He'll hang if I ever find him," said the earl. "They tried to kill her. The coincidence that I happened to arrive at this inn at the right moment seems the only true one in the whole affair." He fell silent, watching Freddie's sleeping face.

Too many coincidences, the earl was thinking. Lady Rennenord's brother had recommended Captain Cramble. Lady Rennenord had recommended the seminary.

"You were obviously very worried about my ward's welfare," said the earl at last. "Why did you come here without consulting me first, Miss Manson?"

"I did not like to trouble you, my lord," Miss Manson answered hesitantly. "You see, I thought I might be imagining things and . . . and I thought it would do no harm to just check. I'm glad I came. They had her locked up in the coal cellar. They told her you had written saying you did not want her back for the Easter holidays, and after a while she did not believe them and demanded to see your letter. They . . . they beat her, and she broke the rod and threw it in Miss Mary's face."

"How did you find she was in the coal cellar? I am sure no one told you."

So Miss Manson told him about dressing as a gypsy and waiting on the heath to waylay the girls.

The earl looked at Miss Manson's long, rather sheeplike face and gave her a warm smile. "You will be amply rewarded, Miss Manson. I have neglected my young ward in a most shameful way. I think it would be best if I took her to town," he said, half to himself. "A few balls and parties are what she will need to make her forget this nightmare."

"Oh, that would be lovely," said Miss Manson, clasping the book she was reading to her thin chest. "I can imagine it all. She will dazzle all the *ton* and marry a duke!"

The earl looked doubtfully at the book Miss Manson was clutching and wondered whether it was a novel.

"So long as she enjoys herself, there is no need for her to marry yet," he said. "She is much too young to be thinking of marriage."

"Nonsense . . . I mean, I beg your pardon, my lord, but Frederica is nearly nineteen."

"So she is," he mused. "I had forgot."

Miss Manson looked at his handsome face bent with concern over Freddie's sleeping one and said suddenly, "You would not consider marrying her yourself, my lord?"

He raised his thin eyebrows in haughty surprise. "I am on the point of proposing to another lady, Miss Manson. Furthermore, Miss Armstrong is much too young for me."

Lady Rennenord, thought Miss Manson gloomily. How glad I am that I did not say anything! How foolish men are.

But the mere thought of Lady Rennenord brought a frown to the earl's eyes. His beloved was going to have to answer a great number of questions.

Freddie stirred and opened her eyes. She smiled shyly at the earl and held out her hand. He enfolded it in his own and looked down at her, a strange expression in his eyes.

"You are not angry with me?" whispered Freddie. "I am a great deal of trouble to you."

"Not in the slightest," he said gently.

"And will you send me away again?"

He looked down into the pleading blue eyes and held her hand in a firmer clasp.

"Never," he said.

"Are you affianced to Lady Rennenord?"

"No."

"Do you intend to be?"

"What a lot of questions you and Miss Manson do ask. All you need to do is lie there and get strong and dream of all the balls and parties I am going to take you to. You are going to have a Season in London."

"Oh, my lord, thank you."

"I must find some female relative to chaperone you," said the earl thoughtfully, turning over her small hand and looking at the palm like a fortuneteller.

Freddie's eyes slid over to where Miss Manson was sitting. "Would not Miss Manson be suitable?" she ventured. "That is, if she would care for the post of chaperone. She is so brave, Lord Berham, and so very kind. I might have been dead had she not helped me."

The earl looked at Miss Manson in surprise. She was shabby-genteel yet undoubtedly a lady. Freddie had suffered enough from strangers. Let her have someone she liked.

"Well, Miss Manson?" said the earl.

"Oh! Oh! Oh!" said Miss Manson. "I would like it above all things. I —"

Her face fell, and her eyes filled with tears.

"What is the matter?" cried Freddie. "Don't you want to come? Have you changed your mind?"

"It's just that my wardrobe is so very skimpy and . . ."

"A new wardrobe will be supplied. As grand as you wish, Miss Manson," said the earl. Miss Manson looked at him with a beatific smile on her face and then slowly slid from her chair in a dead faint.

"Women!" groaned the earl. "No, stay where you are, Freddie. I know exactly what to do. My life has been plagued with fainting women."

While he ministered to Miss Manson, Freddie lay in a colored, joyful dream of entering a London ballroom on his arm.

But he had called her Freddie, a boy's name.

Freddie all at once thought of Lady Rennenord and felt a shiver of apprehension run through her body.

Chapter 6

Lady Rennenord paced up and down the room in a greater state of agitation than her brother had ever seen her in before.

"And I had to pay that fool Cramble five hundred pounds!" raged Clarissa Rennenord. "I told him he had made a mull of the affair, and he said if I did not pay him, then he would go to Lord Berham and tell him the whole thing."

"Well, you should have told him to do just that," said Harry pettishly. "You told me he tried to drown the girl. The man wouldn't dare show his face near Berham Court. And how are you to get out of this pickle, Clarissa? I find Cramble as a tutor, Cramble subsequently tries to kill Frederica. *You*, my sweeting, speak highly of this seminary, which turns out to be a prison for unwanted daughters.

"The whole matter has reached the London newspapers, and Berham has sworn vengeance on those two women. Cramble is a wanted man, and any day, unless you play your cards aright, *you* are going to be a wanted woman. That Manson female was there. Do you think she has told the dear earl of your visit?"

"Not if she knows what's good for her," said

Lady Rennenord sourly. "If only Berham would propose. I would insist on an early marriage, and after that is achieved, anyone can tell him anything they like."

She paced up and down, the silk of her train sweeping the floor.

"Can't you sit down?" said Harry plaintively. "You're making my head ache. Anyway, what do you want to marry Berham *for?* You've got pots and pots of money. Rennenord left you well off. You sold his mansion and all his racehorses, and now you only pay the Bellisle woman a pittance for your keep."

"I want more," said his sister, her eyes flashing. "Don't you know Berham is one of the richest men in England? And he is a leader of the *ton.* I do not wish to stagnate in the country all my life! I need just a little more time."

She continued her pacing while her brother watched her nervously. At last her face cleared, and she sat down.

"I think I have it," she said slowly. "You must go to Lamstowe with a letter from me. Tell the earl you learned that Cramble had a spite against the girl after his dismissal. You met him in a coffeehouse and inadvertently told him that *Frederick* Armstrong was at Lamstowe. He must have come upon her by chance. That is what you must say. You must be abject. I will plead innocence. As long as he has not found that letter I wrote to Cassandra Hope, then I am safe. He *cannot* have found it or I am sure I should have heard from him by now. Wait! I will come with you. It is a risk to leave him sequestered in a country inn with that minx. I shall tell him Mrs. Haddington highly recommended the seminary.

"After all, she is all that is respectable, and all these parents are swearing blind they did not know what an awful place it was when of course they must be lying in their teeth. He *must* be made to believe me. Tell Mrs. Bellisle we are taking the traveling carriage. And *hurry!*"

Freddie was blissfully happy. It was her first day out of doors, and the earl was driving her in his curricle with Miss Manson sitting bodkin between them. The remaining rooms at the inn had been taken up by the arrival of several of the earl's servants. There was a maid for Freddie and a valet for the earl. Four tall footmen had arrived to act as bodyguards.

The earl had mysteriously managed to conjure up new clothes for Freddie and Miss Manson. In vain did Miss Manson protest that she had her own clothes with her. The earl insisted that she must be dressed suitably for her new role of chaperone.

A generous salary had been agreed on. Miss Manson now wished heartily that she had told the earl of Lady Rennenord's visit. But if she told him at this late date, he might think her a sly and untrustworthy person — and Miss Manson longed to go to London.

Like most shy people, her world was filled with hanging judges, all ready to condemn her for her sins, and so she still said never a word. She was also very much in awe of the aristocracy in general and the earl in particular. Although she admired him immensely, she still regarded him nervously as a sort of Greek god, bestowing favors which he might withdraw erratically at any moment.

They drove up over the cliffs and past the school. The earl asked Freddie if she would not like to visit her former companions, but the idea of even setting foot in the place made her turn quite white and begin to tremble. She did not relax until they had driven past and the mansion was lost to view.

Despite the sunshine, both ladies were warmly dressed in their new finery, for there was a chill wind sending clouds scudding across the sky and whipping up white horses on the dark blue water.

Freddie was wearing a brown pelisse edged with soft gray fur. A pale green silk bonnet sat jauntily on her shiny curls and was tied under her chin with a brown silk ribbon.

Miss Manson felt transformed in a bottle-green velvet coat over a white lawn gown. The coat was frogged. The maid had curled her hair in the latest fashion and had placed a velvet hat with curled ostrich plumes on top of her head. But Miss Manson could not help hoping that one day she would feel fashionable *inside* as well as out. She still felt like a retired schoolteacher masquerading as one of the quality.

"You are very kind to squire us like this," she heard Freddie say, "but no doubt you wish you were back at Berham Court."

"On the contrary." The earl laughed. "I am very content. I have the company of a pretty young girl and a distinguished lady. What more could a man ask?"

Freddie looked up at him with laughing eyes, and he turned for a moment and looked down at her, his rather harsh face softened by tenderness.

Why, I believe he might fall in love with her! thought Miss Manson. And Frederica is beginning to *flirt* with him.

Freddie was saying, "Do you think you will find someone to marry me this Season, my lord?"

"No," he said with a sudden frown. "You are much too young and too unused to the ways of the world."

"But perhaps I might find an older man to guide me," Freddie suggested, peeping up at him from under the shadow of her bonnet.

"We will see how you 'take,' " he said with a laugh. "Red hair is not at all fashionable, you know. The duke of Wellington dislikes red hair so much that he went to the length of shaving his son's eyebrows. Just think, Miss Frederica! He will rush upon you in Almack's, brandishing his razor."

"Oh," said Freddie in a disappointed voice. "Perhaps I could dye my hair."

"No, don't do that," he said seriously. "It is the most wonderful color of red. It burns like a flame above the whiteness of your skin and the sapphire of your eyes."

"My lord!" said Freddie, blushing. "You are teasing me."

"Perhaps," he said lightly.

Freddie stole another look at him, but he was giving all his attention to his team.

She had never seen him in the slightest disheveled, thought Freddie. He must have looked a mess after he had pulled her out of the water, but all she could remember was opening her eyes and seeing the beloved stern lines of his face and knowing that she was safe.

Suddenly the whole idea that she was indeed safe at last, and cared for, warmed Freddie's heart, and all the pain of loneliness and homelessness began to ebb away.

They were clattering down the cliff road which led to the edge of the town in which the Duke of Marlborough was situated. Freddie braced herself back against the seat as the horses negotiated the steep hill. Directly below she could see the long arm of the harbor jutting out into the sea. Down on the quay, fishermen were gathering in groups, preparatory to setting out for the night's fishing. Smoke rose in the air from cottages. The wind had died down as it usually and mysteriously does at the turn of the tide, and everything was very still.

A lady and a gentleman were promenading by the harbor wall, the lady's gown a bright splash of color against the gray of the old stone.

"I must be dreaming," said Freddie aloud. "That looks remarkably like Lady Rennenord."

"It is," said the earl.

Freddie's golden day shivered and broke into a thousand fragments.

"Go into the inn with Miss Manson," said the earl shortly.

He helped both ladies to alight and then strode over to where Lady Rennenord was standing with her brother.

She looked like a fashion plate, thought Freddie bitterly. Freddie had been feeling quite a lady of the world until she set eyes on Lady Rennenord, who was wearing a dark blue velvet redingote over a pink gown which fell in ruched flounces to her diminutive feet. Her pink felt hat was bound with dark blue satin ribbons, producing a sort of three-tier effect. The brim was small, and the hat was cut higher at the back, revealing a Grecian knot of glossy brown ringlets.

Her huge pansy-brown eyes looked enormous in her porcelain face. Her mouth was deliciously small. Freddie unconsciously primped up her own generous mouth, thinking sadly that everything that could be unfashionable *was* unfashionable about her own appearance. Her mouth was too wide, her hair was too red, and her bosom was too small.

The earl bent his dark head to kiss Lady Rennenord's hand, and Miss Manson tugged urgently at Freddie's sleeve and led her into the inn.

But Freddie could hardly wait to get upstairs so that she could look out and see what was happening and torture herself further. By the time she pushed open the casement window of her room, the three appeared to be engaged in heated conversation. Miss Manson had explained that the gentleman with Lady Rennenord was her brother. Freddie saw him passionately strike his breast, all his gestures exaggerated like those of an actor.

By contrast, Lady Rennenord was cool and poised. Then Harry turned and strode away, and the earl and Lady Rennenord walked slowly side by side, up and down beside the darkening sea.

"So you see, my dear Lord Berham," Lady Rennenord was saying, "it has all been the most horrendous mistake. How was I to know that Haddington female was such a monster? I was appalled when the news reached me."

"How did the news reach you?" asked the earl, stopping and turning to face her, his dark eyes raking her face.

She turned her limpid gaze up to his face. "Why, Mrs. Haddington wrote to me, of course," she lied. "How else would I know? She told me she had no idea the seminary was such a dreadful place. They were by the way of stopping letters, you see. But her daughter, Jane, had managed to smuggle one out."

"Strange that Jane should manage to inform her parents about the school at the same time Freddie made her escape."

"Exactly," said Lady Rennenord without a blush. "And then, of course, when we arrived in the town, well, it was abuzz with all the news. I was fortunate to have arrived when I did."

"There is really nothing you can do now," said the earl curtly.

"Oh, but there *is!* I must apologize to Miss Armstrong. You must see that. Oh, do not look at me *so.* You are making me feel like a wicked and unfeeling woman, and . . . and it has all been a terrible mistake."

Lady Rennenord turned away and began to cry.

"Don't," said the earl in a much softer voice. "I cannot bear to see you in such distress. It is my fault. I should have cared better for my poor ward. But I will make it up to her. I am taking her to London for the Season. She inherits a considerable fortune when she is twenty-one, and so she is by way of being an heiress. It will not be difficult to find suitors for her. It will be a question of finding the *right* suitor."

"She will need some lady to present her," said Clarissa Rennenord quickly, drying her eyes.

"As to that, I shall escort her myself, and Miss Manson has offered to stand as chaperone."

"Miss Manson! Surely, Lord Berham, you can find someone more suitable."

"I find Miss Manson very suitable," he said quietly. "She has been extremely brave. Do you know the poor woman even went to the lengths of dressing up as a gypsy so that she could find out about Frederica? I am deeply indebted to her."

Lady Rennenord bit her lip. A deeply indebted Lord Berham meant a generous Lord Berham. A Miss Manson with money meant a Miss Manson who would talk. She had not done so yet, obviously. The whole future seemed full of people who might gossip to Lord Berham.

"I am so miserable," she said softly. "I feel that you are angry with me, that you do not trust me."

She turned towards him, her whole body pliant and pleading, and the earl felt his senses quickening. How could he think badly of someone so fair and delicate?

"Of course I trust you," he said. "You have been a victim of circumstances, that is all. Tell your brother to see me. He must tell me all he knows about Captain Cramble so that I may get him arrested as soon as possible. There is no need for you both to stay at Lamstowe. I will convey your apologies to Frederica. She has probably retired to bed. This was her first day on her feet. The blow to her head has healed miraculously, but she is still weak."

I must see Miss Manson, thought Clarissa nervously.

"Perhaps we will stay a day or two," she said.

"It is a picturesque spot, and Harry and I are in need of fresh air. I will only spend a little time with Miss Armstrong, but I should sleep easier tonight if I knew she forgave me."

She swayed slightly towards him, her eyes enormous in the gathering dusk. Her lips were trembling slightly, and her face was tilted towards his own. He bent his head.

A loud scream came from the direction of the inn.

"Frederica!" cried the earl. "Excuse me."

He ran full tilt towards the inn. Lady Rennenord hurried after him, muttering a very unladylike oath under her breath.

The earl took the stairs three at a time and crashed into Freddie's bedroom.

She was sitting beside the window, looking very neat and composed. Miss Manson was knitting quietly in a corner.

"What on earth happened?" demanded the earl, looking about wildly as if expecting to see Captain Cramble lurking in one of the shadowy corners.

"I *am* sorry I startled you," said Freddie sweetly. "I thought I saw a mouse."

"It's all right," said the earl to his servants, who were crowding the doorway. "Miss Armstrong has come to no harm."

He walked over and shut the door and then crossed to the window. It would afford a perfect view, he thought, of where he had been standing with Lady Rennenord.

"So you were frightened by a mouse, Frederica?" he said, pulling forward a chair and sitting down next to her. "You thought nothing of breaking up a cockfight, and yet you scream at the thought of a mouse! Come, Freddie, you can do better than that."

"Indeed I did, my lord," Freddie protested, not meeting his gaze.

He hitched his chair closer and said in a low voice which reached only her ears. "Hear this, Frederica Armstrong. I will brook no interference in my affairs."

Freddie opened her mouth to reply when there came a gentle knocking at the door. "Come in!" she called, glad of the interruption. Lady Rennenord drifted in.

Lord Berham rose to his feet. "Miss Frederica thought she saw a mouse," he said.

"I am terrified of mice myself." Lady Rennenord smiled. Freddie turned her small head away and looked mulishly out the window.

Lady Rennenord fluttered forward and knelt at Freddie's feet. "My dear Miss Armstrong," she said huskily, "please forgive me. I am tortured with guilt. Had I known how dreadful the seminary was, then I should *never* have recommended it. Oh, please say you forgive me!"

Freddie looked down at her, her own face quite blank. What a beautiful picture Lady Rennenord made! And how well aware she was of it, thought Freddie nastily. But to refuse the apology would be to end up at odds with Lord Berham.

Freddie smiled sweetly and said, "Thank you for your apology, my lady. There is no need to kneel to me. I am sure you recommended the seminary simply because you were prompted by your usual . . . er . . . pure motives."

Lady Rennenord smiled graciously upon her and rose to her feet. But the earl had caught the tinge of sarcasm in Freddie's voice and scowled at her from the other side of the room.

"And now I had better find my brother," said Lady Rennenord gaily, shaking out her skirts in such a way as to reveal tantalizing glimpses of ankle.

"Perhaps you will walk with me for a little," she went on, looking in Miss Manson's direction. "The air is still quite warm."

Miss Manson hesitated, but Freddie was too upset and angry, and the earl seemed to find nothing amiss with the suggestion.

Miss Manson reluctantly nodded and picked up her bonnet. She knew exactly why Lady Rennenord wished to speak to her.

Oh, how Miss Manson longed to be free of the threat of poverty, to tell Lady Rennenord to go jump in the sea!

Miss Manson had once been employed briefly as companion to a very wealthy lady, a Mrs. Yarwood. She had endured Mrs. Yarwood's bullying and temper tantrums simply because she had no other hope of employment, and despite the miserable pittance Mrs. Yarwood paid her, Mrs. Yarwood had promised to leave her a substantial amount in her will. But Mrs. Yarwood had died and had left everything to a nephew she hadn't seen in years. Destitution again had stared Miss Manson in the face.

The job at the seminary in Berham had been like a lifeline. Again, the wages were small. When the seminary had closed, then had come the unexpected allowance from the trust of a long-forgotten relative and Mrs. Bellisle's offer of the cottage at a nominal rent. Miss Manson was able to grow vegetables in her garden and keep a few chickens. Now she was employed again. But what if Frederica should marry during her first Season? Frederica was a darling, but she was young, and the young were heedless and knew nothing of the rigors of genteel poverty.

Miss Manson's cottage was the first and only home she had ever known since the death of her parents, twenty years ago.

All these thoughts raced through her head as she walked out of the inn with Lady Rennenord.

"I gather you did not mention my little visit to Lord Berham," Lady Rennenord began when they had walked some way from the inn.

"No, my lady, I did not think it was necessary."

"Very sensible of you," murmured Lady Rennenord. "I was in a terrible predicament, as you will well be able to understand. I innocently recommended the seminary in good faith. I did not want Lord Berham upset by your tales. You must forgive me, Miss Manson. I thought you were exaggerating. I am truly grateful to you for your rescue of Miss Armstrong."

"I did not really rescue her," said Miss Manson gruffly. "She escaped herself. I was merely there to meet her."

"But she is very dear to Lord Berham, is she not?"

Miss Manson took her cue. "He feels a great deal of responsibility for Miss Armstrong. It sometimes weighs heavily on him, I think."

Lady Rennenord brightened perceptibly and took Miss Manson's arm in a friendly grasp. "Why, then, the sooner she is married, the better. But you should have told me you planned to go to Lamstowe," she chided gaily, although Miss Manson detected an underlying threat in the words.

"I felt you would think I was being silly," Miss Manson replied mildly.

"But now you know that I have Miss Armstrong's best interests at heart, I feel sure you will inform me in future of anything that troubles you."

"Of course."

Lady Rennenord squeezed her arm. "You will not find me ungenerous, Miss Manson. I will walk back with you."

They turned about, heading back towards the inn, with Lady Rennenord feeling reassured and Miss Manson feeling small and grubby and cowardly. The earl was waiting for them outside the inn.

"I wish a word in private with Lady Rennenord," he said to Miss Manson. "I think Frederica should be in bed. See if you can persuade her to go."

When Miss Manson left, he turned to Lady Rennenord. "Did Mr. Struthers-Benton tell Captain Cramble that Frederica was a girl?"

"Oh, no, my lord," she said, telling the lie with the ease of long practice.

"But you told your brother?"

"Yes, Lord Berham. Alas, I did tell him. In my great agitation of spirit over the matter of the seminary, I fear I did. But I swear I shall not tell a soul, and neither will Harry."

"It is strange indeed that Cramble came here."

"Well, he was bent on revenge, and if he had called at Berham Court or even in the town, it would have been easy to find out from one of your servants."

"I have sworn them to secrecy," said the earl, frowning, "and all are loyal to me."

"I have never met a servant yet who would not gossip," said Lady Rennenord with some asperity. "Of course, if you prefer to take the word of servants rather than the word of a gentleman . . ."

"I did not say that. I merely wish to make sure that no one ever finds out that Frederica spent anytime under my roof without a chaperone. It is different here with Miss Manson and an innful of servants. Come now," he teased, "you would not wish to see me forced to marry the girl."

"I think it would break my heart," said Clarissa Rennenord in a low voice. She put up her hands and removed her bonnet and then shook her curls so that they tumbled about her shoulders. The gesture was exquisitely feminine. A subtle perfume drifted from her clothes, a faint tantalizing mixture of rose water and musk.

The earl hesitated. Obviously the gentlemanly thing would be to return her sentiment with one equally strong.

Her neck gleamed white in the yellow light of the inn's lamps. Her eyes were mysterious pools of darkness.

Something struck Lady Rennenord on the head and fell at her feet. They looked down. A book lay between them.

"I am *so* sorry," came Freddie's voice from the window above their heads. "It fell from my grasp. Could you please bring it up to me? Good night, my lady."

The earl stooped to retrieve the book, and in that moment, as he bent down, Lady Rennenord looked up at Freddie. Their eyes locked in a mutual stare of hostility.

Harry Struthers-Benton came strolling up, demanding to know whether his sister was going to join him for supper at the other inn.

Lady Rennenord said good night to the earl, searching his face for any signs that he might wish to send Harry to the devil and spend some time alone with her. But his face wore a closed look as he looked at Harry, and he merely bowed in a formal way and made his way into the inn.

He thoughtfully walked into Freddie's room and stood looking down at her. She was sitting up in bed, presenting a very angelic and virginal picture in a white lace nightgown and a jaunty lace cap.

Miss Manson was sitting by the fire, looking miserable.

The earl held up his hand. "Do not apologize, Frederica, for what was a quite deliberate action."

"My lord, I . . ."

"No, do not protest. This is the last time I shall remind you. *Do not interfere.* If I wish to get married, then there is nothing you can do to stop it. If you had taken Lady Rennenord in dislike because of your unfortunate experience at the seminary, then I could well understand it. But you always disliked her, did you not? If we are to become friends, Frederica, then you must not interfere in my life."

"Yes, sir," mumbled Freddie.

He reminded himself she was still ill and said in a softer tone, "Since it appears you are not yet ready to sleep, may I suggest a game of chess?"

Freddie nodded eagerly, so he left the room, to return a few moments later with a chess set and a board, which he placed on the bed. He sat down on the edge of the bed next to Freddie, and the game commenced.

They played silently and amicably for a long time. Miss Manson watched them from time to time, thinking they made a handsome couple and wishing the earl would look at Frederica the same way he looked at Lady Rennenord.

"Checkmate," said the earl at last.

"Oh, no," scowled Freddie. "There must be *some* move I can make."

She moved her legs under the bedclothes, and the board tilted, sending all the pieces scattering over the coverlet.

"Well, that's finished that." The earl laughed, stretching over her to pick up some pawns.

He lost his balance and fell across her. He laughingly pulled himself upright, looking down at her with a mocking, teasing expression on his face while Freddie laughed back at him, face flushed, eyes gleaming with mischief.

The earl took her hand in his and kissed it. "Bedtime for you, miss," he said. Then, still holding her hand, he continued to look at her in a puzzled way.

Suddenly he let her hand drop and strode from the room with an abrupt "good night."

Miss Manson smiled to herself and nodded wisely. But Freddie gazed after him, her face crumpling in disappointment.

"Do you think I angered him, Miss Manson?" she asked. "Do you think he is angry because I knocked over the chessmen?"

"No," said Miss Manson, looking at her with affection. "On the contrary, I think he is well pleased with you."

Miss Manson felt a sudden sharp stab of guilt.

She must tell Freddie to beware of Lady Rennenord, must tell her of that visit.

But the gates of the workhouse seemed to loom before her eyes. She, too, rose abruptly. "Good night, my dear," she said, and hurriedly left the room.

Everyone's cross with me, thought Freddie dismally. What did I do?

Chapter 7

It was a new fashionable court in this new nineteenth-century into which Miss Frederica Armstrong was about to make her debut.

The court circled not around the mad King George or around his son, the fat and florid Prince of Wales, but around that quintessence of dandyism, Mr. Beau Brummell.

At no other time in history could such a personage as Beau Brummell have risen to such heights. After the scares of the French Revolution and the revolt of the American colonies, the aristocrats were recovering from their fears and once again had decided that they were not in imminent danger of being strung up on the nearest lamppost.

Once again they desired to hammer home the barriers that placed them above the common herd, and Mr. Brummell was there to supply them with an exquisite and agonizing set of rules.

Brummell had only his wit and his arrogant superiority to elevate him to the top of the ranks. He had no coat of arms on his carriage; in fact, he didn't even own a carriage. He had no ancestral portraits and no ancestral halls. He had no title other than Mr. Brummell, *arbiter elegantiarum,* or, according to the slang of his peers, "top of the male *ton.*"

To Brummell and his court, all reactions, passions, and enthusiasms were suitable for the vulgar but not for anyone aspiring to be a member of the *ton.*

Once, when an acquaintance was boring Brummell with his raptures about the Lake District and demanded to know which of the lakes the Beau most admired, Brummell sent for his butler, and demanded, "Robinson."

"Sir?"

"Which of the lakes do I admire?"

"Windermere, sir."

"Ah, yes, Windermere," repeated Brummell languidly. "So it is, Windermere."

Enthusiasm of any kind was suspect. It was no longer *convenable* for ladies or gentlemen to exert themselves in any way. The slightest chores must be performed by a servant. Ladies spent hours practicing the art of sitting down in a chair without glancing behind them. One must always assume a footman was at the ready to push a chair under the aristocratic backside, and this little sophistry caused quite a number of nasty falls in households where people had all the social pretensions but none of the footmen to encourage them.

A lady must be prepared to endure the rigors of the English summer dressed in a state of seminudity. Gentlemen must have their coats so exquisitely and tightly tailored that it required the exertions of two strong footmen to get the master into one of them.

Like young wine, the Beau's witticisms did not travel well. To appreciate him saying to a gentleman, "Do you call that *thing* a coat?" one had to be there, in the presence, to see the shrug that accompanied the remark, hear the intonation, see the raised eyebrow. Brummell appealed to the desire of many of the *ton* to be humiliated, in the same way that they allowed their hairdressers to insult them.

It was a cruel world of gossip and slander. Heaven help the debutante who had lost her virginity before she set foot on the Marriage Mart. Somehow the gossip would out. Of course, if the girl had a very large dowry, no one would believe it. One believed the worst only of young misses possessed of indifferent fortunes.

Female society made as much as they could out of the Season, for they were shamefully neglected by the men for the rest of the year. The little dancing and gossiping world of Almack's assembly rooms was the hub of society, and many and bitter were the tears shed by those whose applications were rejected by the despotic patronesses.

The rest of the year, the men vanished onto the hunting field or into politics or into their mysterious clubs, and once more the women were abandoned to their own society. It was the heyday of the six-bottle men, and near the end of a dinner party most of the male — and female — guests were fit for nothing but bed.

The style of beauty with which Lady Rennenord was blessed reigned supreme. Fair hair was considered "unfortunate" and red hair "a disgrace." A beauty of the *ton* must have dark brown hair, a round, dark, soulful eye, a small mouth, a full swelling bosom, and that pearly complexion "which seems to be concomitant with humidity and fog."

Second to the man he had helped raise to the top of the pinnacle of fashion — Beau Brummell — was the Prince of Wales, only but lately appointed Prince Regent, since it was feared King George III would no longer recover from his bouts of madness.

The prince really preferred the company of people he could patronize. He had an unfortunate habit of losing his heart to ladies old enough to be his grandmother. Yet the prince's love of clothes and gossip and fine wine and good food had given society the lead they craved after all that dreadful liberty, freedom, and equality of the last century.

The parade ground of society was Hyde Park, a rural area with entrances from Piccadilly and Oxford Street, with cows and deer grazing under the trees. The company that congregated around five in the evening was composed of dandies and women of the best society as well as ladies of the Fashionable Impure. The dandy's dress consisted of a blue coat with brass buttons, leather breeches, and top boots, and it was the fashion to wear a deep, stiff white cravat which prevented a man from seeing his boots while standing.

There was a much uglier face to London — sprawling slums and dreadful poverty — but if you lived in the West End in a lord's townhouse, as Freddie did, you were insulated from any sight other than society at play.

Freddie was dazzled, bewildered, and nervous. How could she expect to keep such an important man as the earl by her side when there were so many beautiful women about?

She was further troubled by the intelligence that Lady Rennenord was in town. Freddie had been taken driving in the park by the earl. She could not help noticing some of the bold looks that were cast in the earl's direction. She could not help also noticing the scandalous dress of these ladies. She did not know she was looking at some of London's high-class courtesans.

And so the first evening that the earl was to escort Freddie to her very first ball started disastrously.

Miss Manson had allowed Freddie free rein when it came to choice of dress. Freddie had modeled her choice on the gowns of the high-flyers she had seen in the park. Accordingly, when the earl turned around in his drawing room with a smile on his lips to greet his ward, his face froze in horror.

From the zebra-striped feathers in her red

hair to the transparent damped muslin of her gown and down to her painted toenails, Freddie looked more like a Cyprian dressed for a ball at the Argyle Rooms than a young lady attired for a fashionable affair.

He closed his eyes and opened them again. Miss Manson stood nervously behind Freddie. She had felt sure that Frederica's gown was sadly shocking, but then so many society ladies dressed like courtesans.

"How could you?" raged the earl. "You look like the veriest trollop. I am here to present a virginal debutante to the *ton*. Not a . . . a *doxy*."

Freddie's face flamed scarlet.

"Do you realize you are practically *naked?*" her guardian fumed on. "You leave little to the imagination." He pulled out his quizzing glass and stared at the blushing girl from head to foot. "Go and take those things off immediately. Have you no other ball gowns?"

Freddie shook her head miserably.

"Then in that case you will need to stay at home this evening. I am sorry, but you cannot possibly appear like that. I must go myself. Lady Rennenord has no one to escort her to the Spencers' ball. I am already a trifle late."

Freddie let out a choked sob and fled from the room. A moment later he could hear the door of her room bang upstairs.

"I am so sorry," Miss Manson stuttered.

"So am I," he said curtly, drawing his gloves on. "I am surprised at you, Miss Manson. How could you let her buy such things? I will take her with me to Madame Verné tomorrow. She looked the veriest quiz."

Which all went to show, thought Miss Manson dismally as she climbed the stairs to join Freddie, the wisdom of not betraying Lady Rennenord.

Freddie was lying facedown on her bed, weeping bitterly.

She had dreamed of nothing else but this first ball. Time after time she had imagined appearing before the earl in all her finery and seeing the look of love and admiration on his face. Now he had gone off with Lady Rennenord, alone.

"He will probably propose to her," wailed Freddie.

Miss Manson comforted her by nodding gloomily in agreement and then bursting into tears.

"Oh, Miss Manson, do not cry. It will not be as bad as that. Just think! All this time has passed, and he is still unwed."

"There is something I should tell you about Lady Rennenord," said Miss Manson.

"Oh, what can you tell me about her that I don't know already?" said Freddie crossly, jumping from the bed and dashing the tears from her eyes. "If only I could be there all the same, just to spoil her fun."

"Frederica," said Miss Manson desperately, "I really must tell . . ."

"I think I will go to bed," said Freddie abruptly. "Good night."

Miss Manson opened her mouth, but her courage failed her. She trailed miserably from the room.

Freddie listened until her footsteps had died away, and then she locked the door and started rummaging feverishly in closets and drawers. She had not told the servants to throw away her boy's clothes, so they surely must have packed them.

She found them hanging in the back of a large wardrobe in the dressing room which adjoined her bedroom.

There was one fairly good suit of evening clothes, although she always thought they made her look a little like a solicitor's clerk since they were of rusty black silk. She hurriedly changed out of the despised ball gown and into knee breeches and jacket and cambric shirt. The cravat seemed to take an age to tie since she had not been accustomed to wearing boy's clothes since Lamstowe. She searched frantically for her black wig and then remembered leaving it on the harbor wall the night Captain Cramble had thrown the stone at her. Then she saw a box of hair powder on the dressing table and a jar of pomatum.

The servants were all safely in their quarters when Freddie crept down the stairs and through the hall, a slim boyish figure in black coat, knee breeches, white silk stockings, and buckled shoes. Her hair was powdered and tied back at the nape of her neck with a black silk ribbon.

She had been unable to find her sword.

The earl's townhouse was in Berkeley Square, and the Spencers' ball was to be held at Lord Spencer's townhouse, which was situated in Berkeley Street. Thus, Freddie had to walk only a short distance.

Freddie nervously walked up the strip of red carpet which was laid across the pavement, took a deep breath, puffed out her buckram-wadded chest, and walked into the hall.

A large, stately-looking butler swooped down on her. "I wondered where that extra footman I asked the agency for had got to," he growled. "Don't you know better than to enter by the front door? Never mind. Now that you're here, you may as well come along with me to the refreshment room and I'll give you your duties."

Freddie was about to protest that he had made a mistake, that she was, in fact, one of the guests, when she caught a glimpse of her appearance in a long looking glass in the hall. She looked drab and shabby. A group of young men crossed the hall, and the light winked on their jewels.

Freddie meekly followed the butler. At least she was inside. She gazed about her as she followed the butler's broad back, dazzled by the banks of flowers, the glittering jewels, and the beautiful gowns.

If only she could have been here on Lord Berham's arm.

Freddie glanced into the ballroom as they passed one of the entrances to it. Lord Berham was performing a Scotch reel with Lady Rennenord. Lady Rennenord was in white silk and diamonds. She looked beautiful and radiant; the earl looked enchanted.

"Come along, lad," snapped the butler over his shoulder, "and stop gawking like a rustic."

He led the way into the refreshment room and turned Freddie over to the care of the first footman, who was called John.

John was over six feet tall and as haughty as one of the patronesses of Almack's. He looked down his long nose at Freddie's slight form and sighed. "Don't know what the agencies think they're sending us these days. You'd best do something simple. This is by way of what we calls a boofy. They comes along and fills their plates. They points to various things, and we gives 'em what they points to.

"Now, this here is a bowl o' negus for the ladies." He indicated a large silver bowl of hot sweetened wine and water which was set on a small spirit lamp with a low flame. "Named after Colonel F. Negus, what invented the plaguey stuff. No wonder he's dead. Rot your guts, that will. Anyways, when madam asks for a glass, you take this ladle here and one of these little glasses here, and you fills it up. Now, you can't go wrong with that, can you?"

Freddie shook her head.

"All right, then. Take your position. They'll be coming in here in a minute."

Very grand balls had as many candles as it was

possible to have, and this was a very grand ball indeed. The refreshment room was a blaze of light. When the earl entered, Freddie resolved to keep her head down. She would not feel impelled to do anything other than serve negus. She should not have come, she chided herself. He would not propose marriage in the middle of a fashionable crowd like this.

The orchestra in the ballroom struck a loud chord, and the music ceased. The doors to the refreshment room were opened by two tall liveried footmen, and the company began to crowd in.

Freddie was kept very busy for the first half hour. Every lady in the company wanted negus. She served and served, keeping her head down and her eyes averted, blessing the fact that society did not notice servants as human beings.

Then she seemed to feel a pair of eyes boring into her, and an all too familiar voice asked for a glass of negus. Freddie served the earl with her head almost buried in her cravat, not daring to look up until he had moved away.

When she finally found the courage to raise her head, she saw the earl seated quite near her at a table with Lady Rennenord. He seemed in high spirits. His normally harsh features were relaxed. Lady Rennenord was sipping negus and flirting with her eyes over her glass.

Freddie was consumed by a terrible and violent rage. Jealousy seared through her.

She bent under the table and fumbled under the leg of one of her breeches for the woolen garter which was keeping her clocked stocking up.

Standing with the garter in her hand, she looked for a missile. A bowl of fruit caught her eye. On top of the bowl was an overripe peach.

Freddie hesitated, appalled at the enormity of what she was about to do. Lady Rennenord said something and leaned towards the earl in such a way that the top half of her voluptuous bosom was exposed. Freddie ground her teeth.

Placing the peach in the garter, she swung it around her head like a sling and let fly.

The peach struck Lady Rennenord full in the face. Peach juice spattered all down the front of her gown as she screamed. Freddie dived under the table and began to crawl on her hands and knees, all down the length of the long table, towards the door and freedom.

Voices were crying for explanations. Suddenly, above the hubbub a man said clearly, "It was that little footman chap who was serving the negus. He slung the peach right at her."

Freddie doubled up, erupted from under the table, and ran for the door. Twisting and turning, avoiding grabbing hands, she bolted down the staircase and dashed out into the night.

She fled as if the devil himself were at her heels. She bolted around the back of the earl's mansion, hearing the chase behind her. Diving into the stables, she ran slap-bang into one of the grooms, Henry.

" 'Ere, wot's all this?" growled Henry, pinning her arms to her sides.

"It's I, Frederica," panted Freddie. "Let me go before they catch me, Henry. I am in such terrible trouble."

"Why, miss!" gasped Henry, picking up a lantern and holding it to her face. "Wot you dressed like that for? You look like you used to, 'fore we was told you was a female."

"I can't answer questions, Henry. Please get me into the house and up to my room without my lord seeing me. If he knows I have been out this night, Miss Manson will lose her employ and my lord will send me away. Oh, Henry!"

"All right, miss," said the groom. "Come along and I'll let you in by the kitchen door."

The kitchen door led directly to the back stairs. Freddie muttered a hasty "thank you" to Henry and darted up to her room.

She tore off her clothes, rolled them into a ball, and threw them out the window into the garden. She brushed as much of the powder out of her hair as she could and then stuffed her tresses up under a nightcap. Into her nightgown, into bed. Just in time.

"Frederica!" The earl's imperative voice sounded from the doorway.

"Mmmm?" came Freddie's mock-sleepy voice.

The earl strode about the room, lighting candles, and then stood and surveyed Freddie, who was blinking owlishly in the light and looking for all the world as if she had just been roused from a deep sleep.

"What's the matter?" she demanded, struggling up against the pillows.

He began to search the room.

"You are frightening me," exclaimed Freddie. "Say something."

"I am looking for a suit of clothes," said the earl grimly. "Do you still have your boy's clothes?"

"In the wardrobe, in the dressing room," said Freddie faintly.

He disappeared into the dressing room and returned with an armful of clothes. "You will not be needing these again," he said. "Now, get some sleep. You are going with me to Madame Verné's tomorrow."

"Very good, my lord," said Freddie meekly.

He flashed her a suspicious look and strode from the room.

His first thought when he heard a description of the footman who had assaulted Lady Rennenord was that Freddie had somehow gained entry to the ball with the sole intention of humiliating his partner. Now he felt ridiculous. It obviously had been the work of some madman.

The evening was ruined. Lady Rennenord had gone home in tears. The earl did not know they were tears of frustration.

Freddie was such a child, he mused after handing the clothes to a footman to burn. It was a pity he was not married. A wife would be a good companion to a young girl.

He thought of Lady Rennenord. When he was actually with her, he felt enchanted by her femininity and beauty. But now, when he was not, he found it hard to think of her with any degree of warmth. Niggling little questions about Captain Cramble and the seminary would begin to surface in his mind.

At last he came to the conclusion that it would be better to put all thoughts of marriage from his mind until he was shot of Freddie.

She had not yet met any young men. First he must get her some suitable clothes.

While Freddie's wardrobe was being prepared, the earl contented himself by taking her during the day to all the sights of London. Soon he found that he was enjoying himself.

Freddie's enthusiasm was infectious, but it was a childlike enthusiasm, and the earl thought of her more and more as a schoolgirl.

Perhaps it was the desire to reward himself with more mature companionship that prompted him again to suggest that Lady Rennenord should be of the party on the evening they were to go to a ball at the duchess of Hadford's.

The Season had not yet begun officially. He had been able to secure vouchers to Almack's for Freddie. He had taken a box at the Italian opera. He had supervised the delivery of Freddie's gowns. In all, he felt he had done very well for the girl.

By diligently asking his friends in the clubs of St. James's about suitable young men in town, he had secured a beau for Freddie's first ball. His choice had fallen on James Cameron, a wealthy young Scot only a year older than Freddie. He was on leave from the wars in the Peninsula. He had a friendly, open manner and a pair of laughing blue eyes.

The earl thought Freddie would be delighted with his choice.

Freddie was privately furious. Her one dream was to walk into a ballroom with the earl on her arm and be the envy of every lady in the room.

On her drives in the park, on her strolls down London's fashionable thoroughfares, Freddie had not seen one man as handsome as the earl.

Perhaps she would have philosophically accepted James Cameron as her partner with good grace had not the earl been escorting Lady Rennenord. Perhaps Freddie would have made up her mind that it was time she seriously grew up and considered the idea of marriage. But some fifteen minutes before she was due to join the earl and Mr. Cameron in the drawing room, after she had been dressed by the maid and coiffured by the hairdresser, Freddie sat at her toilet table, looking at herself in the glass and fighting down the awful realization that she had fallen in love with her guardian.

Maybe it was the sight of her own face and figure, looking very much like a woman at last in all the glory of white spider gauze over a white silver-embroidered silk slip, that brought all these maturing and mature thoughts flooding into Freddie's startled brain.

Her skin was translucent and faintly tinged

with healthy pink. A sapphire pendant hung between her breasts, and small sapphire earrings ornamented her little ears. Sapphires and silk roses formed a kind of coronet on top of her burnished hair.

She looked at herself with wonder. The last remnants of imposed boyishness fled, leaving her a woman about to descend the stairs and join the man she loved more than anyone or anything in the world.

Miss Manson entered and stood watching her, tears welling up in her eyes.

Freddie now seemed very far removed from her. She looked like a wealthy young debutante without a financial worry in the world. And Miss Manson, despite her fondness for the girl, despite her inherent good nature, envied her from the bottom of her heart.

It was Miss Manson's experience that people with money did not understand the fears of people who did not have any. She looked on the generous salary she received for acting as Freddie's chaperone as a brief interlude in a life dogged with genteel poverty. Like most people who had known nothing but hard times, Miss Manson was unable to enjoy the good times when they arrived. Worry about the future and fear of the workhouse had become so ingrained in her that she almost expected Freddie to be engaged before the evening was out and to dispense with her services on the morrow.

Lady Rennenord was someone Miss Manson

could understand better, with her "come to heel or I shall make matters worse for you" attitude. She might be detestable, but in Miss Manson's eyes Lady Rennenord had the merit of being a familiar beast.

"You look beautiful," she said to Freddie, none of her worries showing on her long face.

"You look very fine yourself." Freddie smiled, taking in the glory of Miss Manson's grand turban and purple silk gown.

Freddie all at once wished from the bottom of her heart that Miss Manson, Lady Rennenord, and the as yet unknown James Cameron would disappear like smoke and leave her alone to go to the ball with Lord Berham.

"Shall we go?" said Freddie, and both women, outwardly calm but inwardly churning, made their way downstairs.

The earl was standing by the fireplace with James Cameron and Lady Rennenord when they entered.

There was a small silence. His face went quite blank as he looked at Freddie. She wondered uneasily whether he was about to find fault with her dress again.

" 'Fore George," muttered Mr. Cameron to the earl. "Your ward is beautiful."

"Yes," said the earl.

Lady Rennenord flashed him an anxious glance. She herself had gone to great lengths to dim any attraction that Freddie might have. She, too, had dressed in white, a tunic gown with a gold key pattern. A diamond collar blazed at her neck, and a large, weighty diamond tiara was on her head.

But no jewels of Lady Rennenord could compete with Freddie's glowing innocence and youth. Her blue eyes sparkled brighter than her sapphires as she looked at her guardian.

The earl was magnificent in blue silk evening coat and straw-colored tight-fitting breeches, clocked stockings, and thin dancing pumps ornamented with diamond buckles.

He walked across to Freddie and raised her hand to his lips. "I am proud of you," he said softly. "How I could ever have taken you for a boy for one moment is beyond me."

Freddie smiled mistily up into his eyes.

Lady Rennenord cleared her throat, making a sharp, irritated sound. "You have not yet introduced Miss Armstrong to Mr. Cameron," she said with a slight edge to her voice.

The earl and Freddie continued to look at each other as if there were no other people present.

James Cameron gave a rueful smile at Lady Rennenord and spread out his hands in a gesture of resignation as if to say, "We are superfluous."

"Lord Berham!" Lady Rennenord's voice was sharp with anxiety.

He turned round, and she saw with dismay that he saw her yet did not see her. Then he appeared to bring himself back to the company with a great effort and made the introductions.

Freddie liked James Cameron on sight. He was a powerfully built young man with a sunny smile and an engaging manner. She told herself firmly that she must not try to monopolize her guardian's attention in any way. If he was determined to wed Lady Rennenord, she must stand aside and let him do so.

She mentally bade a sad farewell to the tomboy who had done her best to keep them apart, to the boy who had thrown the peach at Lady Rennenord.

But when the earl put his hand under Lady Rennenord's arm to help her into the carriage, Freddie turned her head quickly away so that no one should see the pain in her eyes.

There was some slight embarrassment as Freddie was presented to the duke and duchess of Hadford, for she swept both of them a magnificent bow, realized her mistake, and colored almost as red as her hair.

The earl had a sudden awful thought. "Do you know how to dance?" he whispered.

"I had a dancing master," Freddie whispered back. "Of course, I was taught the man's part, but I shall simply reverse the roles."

Freddie then gazed rapturously around the ballroom. In a way, she had seen all this magnificence before, but that time she had been mistaken for a temporary footman.

Mr. Cameron led Freddie out to where a set was forming for a country dance. The earl watched anxiously, forgetting Lady Rennenord's presence at his side.

A man asked her for the honor of a dance, and Lady Rennenord looked crossly at the earl, wondering why *he* had not asked her. But his eyes were still fixed on Freddie. She gave a little shrug and moved off with her partner.

Freddie acquitted herself very well, much to the earl's relief. She was now a beautiful woman, he thought. That sword of hers was hidden in his room. Her boy's clothes had been thrown away. Nothing was now left of the frightened but valiant youth who had stopped a cockfight and had escaped those tormenters at the seminary.

At that thought of the seminary, the earl looked in Lady Rennenord's direction. Not for the first time he wondered about her part in it. He had been so determined to overcome Freddie's dislike of Lady Rennenord that he had never really stopped to wonder if Lady Rennenord disliked Freddie.

Her brother, Harry, had said he had searched the whole of England for Captain Cramble, but the earl had now the gossip from the clubs about Harry Struthers-Benton. He was damned as being weak and lazy and shiftless and a deuced bad friend to have.

Despite efforts by the authorities, Miss Mary Hope and her sister, Cassandra, appeared to have disappeared off the face of the earth. Diligent enquiries revealed that Mary Hope had been companion to an old lady who had owned the large house on the cliffs above Lamstowe. On her death, she had left it to Mary Hope. Mary, who was at least self-educated, had summoned Cassandra, who was employed as a housemaid in another residence, and together they had thought up the idea of the seminary.

He all at once saw Freddie looking across the ballroom to where a stout matron was standing behind a fair-haired girl with a rather long red nose.

He found his host at his elbow and asked the duke for the identities of the two females who seemed to be of such interest to his ward.

"Oh, I thought you would certainly know *them*," said the duke. "That's the Haddington female and her daughter, Jane. I read all about that seminary in the newspapers, don't you see. Prison of a place it turned out to be! Ever catch those women?"

"No," replied the earl. "I would never have sent my ward to such as place had not Mrs. Haddington recommended it through a friend of mine."

He made his way over to where Mrs. Haddington was standing with her daughter. Mrs. Haddington gave him a tentative smile which faded quickly when he introduced himself.

"How was I to know what was going on?" she burst out. "It was not as if I didn't visit Jane. But when I arrived, she always said she was happy and did not want to come home."

"But surely her appearance, ma'am," said the earl. "All the girls seemed terribly thin and starved."

"She always was a skinny little thing," said Mrs. Haddington crossly. "Now, what with all the fuss and bother and people looking at me as if I was a sort of Lady Macbeth, I've got to go to all the expense of a Season."

Jane shuffled her feet and looked miserable.

"After all, you sent your ward there," pointed out Mrs. Haddington, eager to share the guilt.

"It so happens I sent Frederica there because you told Lady Rennenord it was an excellent establishment."

"I didn't quite say that," said Mrs. Haddington. "I told her once that I had sent Jane there because it was a sort of place of correction for young ladies. She knew it was a place for bad girls. Of that I am sure."

"I am sure you are mistaken, ma'am," said the earl haughtily. "Lady Rennenord is extremely fond of my ward and would not do anything to cause Frederica distress." But even as he spoke, he realized that this was far from true. At the same moment he wondered why he had not been aware of the fact before.

"Oh, really?" said Mrs. Haddington spitefully. "She knew very well it was a home for wayward girls. My Jane tried to burn the house down."

"Mama," said Jane miserably.

"Oh, well, she's back with me, and I'd best do

what I can. But don't try to tell me Lady Rennenord didn't know what sort of seminary it was. Of course, I didn't know about their villainy, keeping the money I sent Jane and all that. But my lady *did* know it was a place you sent bad girls."

"I would like to speak to Frederica, please," mumbled Jane.

The dance had just finished. Frederica came up and embraced Jane, and the two girls moved a little away and began to talk in low voices.

The next dance was announced while the earl stood chatting with James Cameron and trying to ignore Mrs. Haddington's presence. While he talked to James, the earl saw Clarissa Rennenord glance quickly in his direction, immediately avert her eyes when she saw Mrs. Haddington, and move quickly away to the opposite end of the long ballroom.

He remembered with dismay that he had engaged to take her to a *fête champêtre* in the Surrey fields the next afternoon. He had already suggested to James earlier in the evening that the young man might oblige him by taking his ward driving so that the earl would be free to court Lady Rennenord.

Now he said, "Mr. Cameron, I had forgot that my ward is included in the invitation to the Oakleys' *fête champêtre* on the morrow. I see Mrs. Oakley in the ballroom and will ask her if I can include you in my invitation."

"I would like it above all things," said James,

his eyes on Freddie's face. "Your ward is enchanting."

"Thank you," said the earl bleakly.

The next dance was announced, and the earl asked Jane to partner him. Freddie was quickly surrounded by a crowd of admirers. The wallflowers might pass acid remarks about how dreadful, how *farouche,* it was to have red hair, how simply too monstrous bad *ton,* but no one seemed to have told the gentlemen around Freddie that sad fact, and if they had, the gentlemen had all obviously forgotten it.

The earl thought as he danced with Jane that he ought to be feeling elated at Freddie's success. Apart from that awkward initial mistake of bowing to her hosts instead of curtsying, Freddie had behaved impeccably.

After the dance was over and he was promenading with Jane, he took the opportunity to ask her how she fared.

"Very well," said Jane with a nervous look in her mother's direction. "Ma got such a hard time in the newspapers that she durst not send me away again."

"I am sure she really wants you at home," said the earl.

"Oh, no, she don't. But I don't care," said Jane, tossing her head. "I'm used to her not liking me."

"What of your father?"

"Dead."

"I'm so sorry."

"Don't. He didn't like me either," said Jane casually.

The earl looked down at her curiously. "Did you *really* try to burn your home down, Miss Haddington?"

"Oh, yes," said Jane. "They didn't ever seem to notice me, you see. It was a lovely fire."

"No one was burned to death, I trust?" remarked the earl acidly.

"No, I'm not *that* wicked. I gave 'em all the alarm in good time. Then the Sun Life Insurance paid out a large sum, and Ma was able to get all new furniture, so I can't understand why she got so upset."

The earl shuddered to think of what his Frederica would have become had she spent two whole years in such company.

Then he reminded himself that he was escorting Lady Rennenord and asked her for the next dance after leaving Jane with her mother. It was a lively Scotch reel, which did not afford opportunity for conversation.

Always he was conscious of Freddie, noticing her popularity, noticing the way men looked at her. After the dance was over, he escaped from his fair partner as soon as he could and asked the duchess of Hadford's permission to dance the waltz with his ward. The waltz had not yet been sanctioned by Almack's, but it was becoming an increasingly popular feature of private dances. Hardly anyone opened a ball with the minuet, something that would have been unthinkable such a short time ago.

Freddie looked up at him wide-eyed. Everyone drew back a little to watch, it seemed, as he took her in his arms and swung her onto the floor. The tall, handsome figure of the earl with his beautiful ward in his arms caused a great deal of speculation.

"It's always the same," said a dowager near Lady Rennenord. "These handsome bucks avoid every snare on the Marriage Mart, and then they tumble head over heels in love with some pretty little thing barely out of the schoolroom."

Panic seized Lady Rennenord. Someone asked her to dance, and she accepted, although she barely knew who had asked her or heard what he had said.

Freddie floated in the earl's arms, dizzy with pleasure, aware of the hard pressure of his hand on the small of her back and his dark, brooding, enigmatic stare as he looked down at her.

It was like plunging into cold water when the music ceased and she found herself handed over to James Cameron while her guardian took Lady Rennenord onto the floor.

Lady Rennenord began to relax. The earl once more seemed interested in her and talked lightly and easily of their proposed outing together on the morrow.

He did not ask Freddie to dance again.

For poor Freddie the whole evening fell flat, and she could only be glad when it was time to go home. Her only small consolation was that

Lady Rennenord did not live with them . . . yet.

The earl drove Lady Rennenord home, and although he refused to enter her house, he said he was looking forward to seeing her at noon the next day and would call for her. With that she was content. Once more, she was sure of him.

Let it only be good weather, she prayed, and I will take him away from the other guests, and he will be able to make his proposal in peace, and then the long waiting will be over. I shall pretend to be fond of that Frederica creature until after the wedding.

Her butler emerged from the shadows of the hall. "Two ladies and a gentleman called to see you," he said in a hushed voice. "I said you would not be back until very late, but they said they would wait. They have some news about Mrs. Bellisle they think you should hear."

Clarissa Rennenord gave a sigh of impatience. That was the trouble with renting a house with its owner's servants for the Season. They really did not seem to know how to go on. Imagine allowing visitors to wait until three in the morning!

"You should have sent them on their way," she said sharply. "Nonetheless, I may as well see them now. Where did you put them?"

"In the little saloon, my lady."

Lady Rennenord walked into the little saloon, which was on the first floor. The butler closed the door softly behind her.

Three figures rose to meet her.

Lady Rennenord let out a sharp cry of alarm.

Facing her were Miss Mary Hope, Miss Cassandra Hope, and Captain Cramble.

Then her first fright disappeared as she realized that they were all wanted by the authorities. They could say what they liked about her in prison.

"Three criminals together." She laughed.

She opened the door and called loudly for the servants.

"You thought to blackmail me again, Cramble," she said over her shoulder. "But you will not find me so naive this time!"

"We will send this letter to the newspapers if you have us arrested," came Miss Mary's assured voice.

"Letter!" Clarissa Rennenord swung round.

Miss Mary held up a long folded piece of paper. "Remember, my lady?" she mocked. "We have your instructions as to what you wanted us to do with Frederica Armstrong. Also your handwritten promise of money if we kept her away from Berham for two years."

The servants came running. "No, it is nothing," Lady Rennenord told them hurriedly. "Nothing at all."

She closed the door slowly and turned to face the three.

"What is it you want?" she demanded harshly. "Money? I have no money here. You will need to wait until the bank opens in the morning. I gather there is no news of Mrs. Bellisle whatsoever."

Captain Cramble gave a jolly laugh. "We do not need money, my lady," he said. "Those jewels you are wearing will do very nicely. None of us has seen Mrs. Bellisle, but it was as good an excuse as any."

Lady Rennenord's hand flew to the diamond collar at her neck. These jewels, the Rennenord diamonds, had been one of the main reasons she had married Lord Rennenord.

"Cannot we sit down and discuss this reasonably?" she pleaded. "I could aid you to leave the country. Everyone has been looking for you. You are all in great peril."

"We have already made arrangements to leave the country. None of *us* wants to marry Berham," leered Cassandra Hope. "Oh, yes, we know your game." She nodded in the direction of the letter her sister was holding. "Perhaps we should take that around to Lord Berham's and leave it for him."

Lady Rennenord turned quite white. Like most not very intelligent people, she was capable of great tenacity. She had set her sights on Lord Berham and meant to bag him if it was the last thing she did. Tomorrow he would propose, of that she was sure.

And then there were the famous Berham diamonds. Mrs. Bellisle had told her about them. So far Frederica had displayed only a few trumpery sapphires. The diamonds would go to the earl's bride. All she needed was a little more time.

"How do I know you will not be back for more?" she asked.

"We ain't silly," said Cassandra. "Once you've got that letter, we can't threaten you."

"Then give it to me!" said Lady Rennenord.

Mary Hope held the letter out of her reach.

"The diamonds," she said.

Lady Rennenord fumbled with the clasp at her neck. "How did you know I would have the jewels?" she demanded. "All my jewels could have been in the bank."

"We watched the house," said Miss Mary, "and we saw you leave. We were wondering how to approach you. We've been watching you for days."

Lady Rennenord shuddered. She loosened the heavy collar and held it out.

Captain Cramble produced a leather bag. Cassandra took the necklace and dropped it in. Next came the tiara.

Mary Hope still held on to the letter tightly. "You will escort us downstairs, my lady," she said. "We will give you the letter when we reach the door. If we give it to you now, you might throw it on the fire and then tell the servants we robbed you."

Lady Rennenord silently led them downstairs. She reached the door first and barred their way.

"Now," she hissed. "The letter!"

Mary placed it in her hand. Captain Cramble opened the street door, and the three criminals disappeared into the night.

Lady Rennenord ran up the stairs as fast as

she could and triumphantly threw the letter on the fire, taking the poker and hitting the curling, blackening pieces of paper again and again until there was nothing left but red-hot ash.

Unaware that she had burned a perfectly blank sheet of paper, she took herself off to bed.

"Well, we've still got the letter," said Captain Cramble, twirling his cane in the air to attract the attention of a cab.

"Yes," gloated Cassandra. "Won't she be mad when we go back for more."

"We're not going back," said her sister. "We're getting out of the country as fast as we can. Only greedy fools go to the same well twice."

They all climbed into a hack. "Berkeley Square," said Miss Mary Hope.

"What we goin' there for?" asked Cassandra.

"To deliver Lady Rennenord's letter to Lord Berham. We shall pay the driver to give it to his lordship's butler. No sense in showing our faces."

"But why?" grumbled Cassandra.

"A farewell gesture," said Miss Mary grandly. "That Lady Rennenord is an evil woman."

"And who should know better than you!" said the captain cheerfully. "It takes one to recognize one, eh, what?"

He was sitting between the sisters, and although the carriage was dark, he could see the shine of their eyes as they both turned and looked at him steadily.

Captain Cramble clutched the bag of diamonds more tightly and felt a faint shiver of fear.

Chapter 8

Lady Rennenord was surprised to be woken by her maid at the unearthly hour of nine in the morning with the intelligence that Lord Berham had called and was waiting below stairs.

He was not supposed to call for her until noon.

She had had only about four hours of sleep. She had not left the ball until three in the morning, and the subsequent excitement of her night visitors had kept her awake until five.

Calling for her lady's maid, she scrutinized her face anxiously in the glass. Faint wrinkles were showing at the edge of her eyes, and the skin under her chin looked a little slack.

But at least she knew she had nothing to fear. That terrible letter was so much cold ash in the grate.

It took her an hour to be satisfied with her appearance. By the time she had finished dressing, her bedroom was a mess of scattered and discarded clothes and her maid was in tears.

Lord Berham was in the library, a little-used room downstairs. The air felt musty and stale. Lady Rennenord frowned over the stupidity of these town servants, curtsied to Lord Berham, and murmured that they would be more comfortable in the morning room.

She kept glancing at his face for some sign as to the nature of his call. It looked harsh and grim and preoccupied.

Becoming increasingly nervous, she sat down in the morning room and smiled up at his hard face.

"And to what do I . . ." she began.

Her voice trailed away as he held an open letter in front of her eyes. It was the one she had sent to the seminary, the one she thought she had burned the night before.

"This was delivered to my butler, madam, shortly before dawn. I await your explanation."

If Lady Rennenord had forced herself quite simply to say that the letter was a forgery, he might have believed her. She was unaware that in her guilt and distress she looked very pretty and feminine. And Miss Mary and Miss Cassandra Hope had proved themselves wicked and un-trustworthy and a pair of consummate liars. The expression of his face was already softening as he looked down on her as she sat there in a lavender gown with multiple flounces and tucks and satin ribbons. A subtle perfume was drifting from her. She had rehearsed every seductive movement for so long and so well that she performed all the little tricks unconsciously, even in her distress. The rapid breathing accentuated the rise and fall of her bosom. The barely withheld tears made her eyes large and luminous. The trembling mouth looked infinitely appealing.

Then the whole delicious confection seemed to harden, to draw itself together into a rigid matron in a state of badly feigned outrage.

"I do not need to explain my actions to you, Lord Berham," she said coldly. Lady Rennenord believed that all hope was lost, and she was rapidly becoming vindictive. This never would have come about if he had just proposed in the first place instead of shilly-shallying like a schoolboy.

Still, he could not quite believe her to be guilty.

"I demand an explanation," he said. "You took it upon yourself to recommend this seminary for my ward. You appear to have written a dreadful letter. You . . ."

"Shut up!"

Lady Rennenord rose and faced him. "I was merely playing for time until you came to your senses. What was I to do? Of course, I would have sent for Frederica once we were married. But while she was there, you could not see anyone else.

"Think of it. The great earl of Berham falling in love with a schoolgirl. A schoolgirl who tricked him. *She* knew what she was doing when she arrived dressed as a boy. You were *meant* to be compromised."

His face was stiff with disgust. Nothing is deeper and more acid than the fury of a man who finds that he has been paying court to a series of gowns and carefully rehearsed attitudes.

"Do not come near me or my ward again," he said. "I have no intention of marrying *any* woman. This unfortunate episode has only gone to prove what I formerly believed: Marriage is a prison for fools and idiots! Good day to you."

He slammed out of the room.

A few moments later, Harry shuffled in.

"I say, was that Berham?" he asked. "He seemed in a terrible temper."

Clarissa Rennenord shrugged. "The game's up, Harry," she said. She told him of her visit from the captain and the sisters, of the trick with the letter and the loss of her diamonds, of the loss of Lord Berham.

"You amaze me," said Harry. "What a fool you are! Did you never think to open the paper they gave you and look at it? Oh, well, you've got plenty of jewels and money, and you ain't a bad looker, so it's no use crying."

"I am not crying, Harry. I want revenge. You should have heard him going on about how he would never marry."

"Well, there's a way to fix that," said Harry cheerfully.

"How?"

"Tell everyone about how that Armstrong girl was living under his roof dressed as a boy and without a chaperone. He'll think it's his servants gossiping."

"No, he won't. They gossiped freely enough about his ward's arrival when they thought she was a boy. But the minute the masquerade was discovered and he told them to keep quiet, they never breathed a word."

"Does it matter if he knows it is you? You don't owe him any loyalty *now*. See, I'll tell you what happened. Seems when he thought Frederica Armstrong was a boy, he took her to a prizefight at Berham. Cully was fighting Grigson, so all the *ton* were there. Some chaps remarked casually in the clubs that this ward of his looked remarkably like the boy who fainted at the prizefight. 'Must have been her brother,' says I, since you told me not to mention anything in case he thought he had to marry the girl. Now all I have to do is tell these chaps and . . . well, there you are. Society loves a scandal."

"They never quite believe scandal about debutantes with money."

"They will about this one. Haven't you seen the way she looks at Berham? It's obvious she's head over heels in love with him. That means it's crying out to the world that she ain't interested in passing her fortune to any other man at the altar. So they'll gossip like mad."

"I think, perhaps, he might be quite pleased to have his mind made up for him," said Lady Rennenord slowly.

"Oh, he might have been pleased given a few Seasons in Miss Armstrong's company," said Harry. "But he won't like being forced to marry her. He'll be furious. He'll never fall in love with the girl. Once he gets over his fury, at you, he'll realize all the trouble she's caused him."

"Then do it," said Lady Rennenord viciously. "I will talk, too. And I will write to Mrs. Bellisle and tell her that the secret is out and that we can all talk freely. She will tell the whole of Berham."

She smiled at her brother. "I would love to see his face when he realizes he'll have to get married after all!"

At that moment the earl was unaware of the plans being made for his downfall. He was still in a towering rage. He summoned Miss Manson and Freddie as soon as he returned and told them of what he had found.

"I knew she hated me," said Freddie simply. But Miss Manson burst into tears, and all they could make out were disjointed remarks like, "I am a coward . . . so frightened . . . my cottage."

Suddenly the earl remembered visiting Miss Manson to ask about Freddie and Miss Manson saying something about its being a pleasant cottage instead of answering his question.

He signaled to Freddie to be quiet until Miss Manson had recovered. When she had dried her eyes, he said, "You know something, don't you, Miss Manson? Something about Lady Rennenord. And it's got something to do with that cottage of yours. Does she own it?"

"Oh, no, my lord," hiccuped Miss Manson. "Mrs. Bellisle owns it. Oh, I will tell you all. I will be dismissed, but I knew my good fortune could not last. I felt it *here*," she said, striking her breast. She took a deep breath, and the whole miserable story of poverty and fear poured out.

"I knew if I told you about how really horrible the seminary was, then she would get Mrs. Bellisle to evict me. But I did go to Lamstowe," she ended pathetically. "And I did help Frederica to escape."

"And did you not think I would protect you?" demanded the earl.

"No," said Miss Manson. "You see, I thought you had too many great cares and responsibilities to concern yourself with me. But I will not be an embarrassment to you any longer. I will leave this day."

"No, you shall not," said Freddie. "Of course Lord Berham understands. You don't need to be poor to understand. You will stay here with me, and we will go to all the balls and parties."

"You may stay," echoed the earl. "But," he added severely, "you must place your loyalty to Miss Armstrong above all else."

"I would die for her," said Miss Manson. "I kneel to you, my lord, in gratitude."

She suited the action to the words. The earl gave a little sigh and lifted her to her feet. "Spare me these scenes, Miss Manson," he said coldly. "Take Frederica upstairs, and both of you make ready to leave."

After they had gone, the earl sat brooding. His former existence, free of the troubles that women always seemed to bring, seemed like a pleasant landscape never again to be seen.

He decided to spend the day at his club. He

had done enough for Frederica. Let James Cameron escort her!

Freddie tried to hide her dismal disappointment when she learned that he was not to go. She rallied slightly in James Cameron's cheerful company and began to decide that the day might not turn out too badly after all. Her guardian was naturally upset by Lady Rennenord's duplicity and was taking his anger out on everyone about him. He would have recovered by the evening, and then they could be comfortable again.

The day was warm and misty. No sooner had they sat down at tables spread out on the meadows next to a stream than a steady rain began to fall as if someone had turned on a tap.

There were screams from the ladies and shouts from the men as they called their servants to get the carriages ready.

Mr. and Mrs. Oakley suggested that they all repair to their mansion, which was hard by. The party could continue there.

But the bad weather had affected the spirits of the guests, and champagne seemed such a wishy-washy drink on a dreary day.

Society no longer wanted to play and grew restless and malicious. The orchestra which was to perform for the guests had failed to appear, the fires smoked, a chill wind was rising outside, and the hard eyes of the *ton* looked around for some victim on whom to inflict their liverish disposition.

Freddie began to feel after some time that

there was a gossipy feeling of shock, curiosity, and malice directed towards herself.

Quizzing glasses were pointed in her direction, heads leaned together, eyes slid away when they met hers.

James Cameron was talking loudly and cheerfully in her ear about his plans to rejoin his regiment. At last Freddie felt she could bear it no longer and interrupted him by saying, "It must be the weather. I feel out of sorts. I feel everyone is talking about me."

James looked round in surprise. "They're probably all saying what a lucky chap I am," he said jovially. "There's my friend, Captain Jimmy Frazier, signaling me like mad. Excuse me, Miss Frederica. I will just see what he wants."

Freddie nodded and he rose and left. She was sitting at the end of a long table, slightly apart from the rest of the guests.

Miss Manson was at another table at the far end of the room. Freddie turned to engage the lady nearest her in conversation but received a startled haughty stare and then nothing but an excellent view of the lady's lace-covered back.

Freddie prayed that James would soon finish his conversation and return. She looked across to where he was standing with Captain Frazier. He caught her gaze and looked pointedly away, his normally cheerful face set in a mask of distaste.

Something was very badly wrong. Summoning up all her courage and aware of fifty pairs of staring eyes, Freddie got up and walked across the room to where James Cameron was standing.

She put up her chin as he pointedly turned his back on her, and then she rapped him on the shoulder with her fan.

"What is the matter?" she demanded.

At that, he turned slowly round and looked her coldly up and down.

But then the earl miraculously appeared at Freddie's side. He tucked Freddie's trembling hand in his arm.

"It seems I am obliged to you again for entertaining my fiancée," he went on. Freddie gave a little gasp. He gave her arm a warning squeeze.

"Fiancée!" exclaimed James Cameron. "But why didn't you tell me? You said I was to escort your ward."

"So I did. I thought I had told you of my good fortune. You misunderstood me, Cameron. I was merely being civil to a young man so lately returned from the wars. I thought it would please you to be of our party. Colonel Harrison said you knew few people in London and were at loose ends."

Put at a thorough disadvantage, James Cameron blushed and stammered out his thanks.

He presented Captain Frazier. Freddie managed a tolerable curtsy.

Then the earl turned and surveyed the room. He took out his quizzing glass and looked thoughtfully around the sea of staring faces.

"Where is Mrs. Oakley?" he demanded in a languid voice which nonetheless carried to every corner of the room. "It's a deuced miserable day, and I am anxious to take my fiancée home."

Mrs. Oakley came hurrying up. Freddie murmured thanks for the entertainment in a dazed way. A little glow of happiness had started somewhere inside her and was beginning to spread throughout her whole body.

He loved her! What a crazy, mad way to propose. Freddie forgot all about the malice and gossip of the room and hung on to the earl's arm, looking up at him with adoring eyes.

Miss Manson came hurrying up.

"You may stay if you wish, Miss Manson," said the earl. "I shall escort my fiancée home."

He gave her a warning look as she was about to burst into rapturous congratulations. "I think you will understand that we have a great deal to talk about."

Miss Manson had heard the gossip and had hated the party accordingly. She longed to leave but in view of the earl's staggering news decided that she had better stay behind. She contented herself by hugging Freddie warmly.

Freddie sailed out on the earl's arm, only dimly aware of the faces about her. The wind sighed in the trees outside and shook heavy raindrops onto the lawns. In the carriage she turned a bright and shining face up to the earl's and then quailed before his look of fury.

"Don't you want to marry me?" she asked. "You look so fierce."

"No, of course I don't want to marry you," he snapped, looking straight ahead and therefore missing the flat, blank look of utter despair on Freddie's face.

"I called at my club after you had left. It was alive with gossip. It appears your resemblance to the youth I took to the prizefight had been remarked on. Now everyone appears to know that you and that youth are the same person and that you were under my roof without a chaperone, dressed as a boy. I could not find who had started the rumor, but Harry Struthers-Benton had left the club ten minutes before I arrived. He and his sister move quickly. Was nothing said to you at the Oakleys'?"

"No, but it was terrible. They were all staring at me and whispering. And just before you arrived, Mr. Cameron cut me."

"Of course he did." The earl gave a harsh laugh. "He must have been outraged. He must have thought I was palming off my used wares on him."

"No!" said Freddie, putting up her hands to her hot cheeks.

"I arrived in time to salvage what I could of the situation. Now that we are to be married, the scandal will die out."

"But I don't want to marry you, since you don't want me," said Freddie, becoming as furious as she was miserable. "Have you no thought for my feelings? Did you never consider that I might have dreamt of marrying someone nearer my own age?"

"What we wished or did not wish for does not enter into this," he said. "I am not having the name of Berham brought down into the mud. I am not in my dotage. What is this about dreaming of a young man? Had you formed a *tendre* for James Cameron?"

"*Yes!*" Freddie lied furiously.

"Forget him," he said abruptly. "He obviously believed the first breath of scandal about you. I would not believe wrong of any woman I loved."

"Obviously," said Freddie dryly. "It's a wonder Lady Rennenord did not cut my throat before you saw her for what she was. Men are such fools. How could you be so taken in by that simpering smile and all those pretty tricks?"

"Perhaps having to look at an excuse for a female who wore boy's clothes gave me a craving for femininity. Now I am to be tied for life to a silly girl who is more than likely to challenge one of the patronesses of Almack's to a duel."

"You should have married Clarissa Rennenord," said Freddie bitterly. "That is exactly the sort of thing she would say."

"All this sparring is vulgar," he said with a weary sigh. "We are to be married as soon as possible, and that is that. I do not expect you to fulfill your marital functions. No doubt you have an ineradicable disgust of that side of marriage, thanks to your grandfather's weird determination to introduce you to the facts of life in as brutal a manner as possible."

Freddie fell silent. Did the earl not realize that if you loved someone as much as she loved him, fears of brutal lust seemed a world apart?

He glanced down at her and said in a kinder voice, "We should not be quarreling like this. You will find you are able to have a pleasant life. I will not interfere with your pleasures. Married women have a great deal of freedom."

"Do you plan to take a mistress?"

"No. Not at this moment."

"Perhaps later? Then what would you say if I took a lover?"

"Fustian!"

"Well, I shall," said Freddie, all her disappointment and rage erupting again. "And we'll see how you like *that!*"

"Don't be childish," he said wearily. "I have enough to worry me without coping with your tantrums."

"And just what do you think you are indulging in, sirrah? A noble rage?"

He turned his head away and did not reply.

Freddie held on to her rage and nursed it. She knew that the minute she stopped being angry, she would burst into tears.

They arrived back at Berkeley Square, still in a grim silence. The earl strode off into the library and slammed the door. Freddie stormed off upstairs to her room.

For a long time she sat and made plans. Then

the door opened, and Miss Manson walked in, her long face radiant.

Freddie held up one small hand. "Before you gush all over me with congratulations, I would have you know that my lord has felt constrained to marry me because of the gossip. He does not love me one little bit."

Miss Manson sat down in a heap on the floor and burst into tears.

Freddie looked at her with some exasperation. "Do not cry," she said. "Please try not to cry. I need help."

Miss Manson took out a handkerchief the size of a young bedsheet and blew her nose. "I feel for you so," she said. "You are so much in love with Lord Berham."

"Does it show so much?" asked Freddie wistfully.

Miss Manson nodded her head. "And he is in love with you," she said.

"Pooh!" Freddie tossed her head. "You should have been in the carriage and heard him fretting and fuming about having to marry me."

"But he looked at you in *such* a way, even at Lamstowe."

"Oh, he is fond enough of me, but he does not love me as a woman. He is furious. It's to be a sort of arranged marriage. I go my way and he goes his. I am planning to run away."

"Where to?"

"To my old home, Hartley Manor. We will go in disguise."

Miss Manson thought about their masquerade at Lamstowe and of how frightened she had been.

"We were to go to see Kean in *Hamlet* this evening," said Miss Manson hopefully.

Freddie frowned, twisting her fan around in her fingers. She had longed to see the famous actor. "But he will be so angry — Lord Berham, I mean."

"Would it not be a good idea to *see?*" ventured Miss Manson. "Very angry gentlemen never stay very angry for long. I will, of course, go with you, Frederica. But I am such a cowardly person that the thought of taking to the road in disguise makes me tremble. Please, could we not go to the play this one evening?"

Freddie thought about seeing the earl again, of sitting next to him at the play.

"Besides," pursued Miss Manson, "there are so many other Lady Rennenords in London who would be only too ready to console him if you disappeared."

"Let them have him!" said Freddie defiantly. But then she capitulated. One more precious evening in his company. Just one.

Just to hear his voice again, watch his satanic dark looks, perhaps hear that husky, caressing note in his voice that he had when he was amused by her.

The earl sat in the library for the rest of the afternoon, brooding savagely on this twist of fate. He forgot how bored he had been before Freddie had crashed into his life. Never had bachelordom seemed so sweet. He thought about the proposed visit to the play. Was this what his life was to be? Escorting a flighty schoolgirl and her eccentric companion? Be damned to both of them. He poured himself another glass of brandy and stared moodily into the flames of the library fire.

Then he heard the faint sounds of someone playing the piano in the drawing room across the hall. Freddie. He had forgotten how well she could play.

After some hesitation he went and opened the library door and listened. She was playing a haunting piece of music which was new to him.

He stood leaning against the door jamb, drinking his brandy and listening. The music sounded sad and wistful, conjuring up nostalgic dreams of lost spring-times and lost youth and wasted passions. He went back into the library and closed the door.

Miss Manson noticed an air of constraint between Lord Berham and Freddie, but at least they did not seem to be quarreling openly as they set out for the theater.

Kean's performance was superb. From his first speech to Rosencrantz and Guildenstern to his distracted speech to Ophelia and his "To be or not to be," he electrified the house. His fencing was magnificent. When he finally fell, the pit rose howling with applause.

Her troubles momentarily forgotten, Freddie turned to Lord Berham. "Wasn't he marvelous?

Many say his Hamlet is inferior to his Richard, but after tonight's performance I cannot believe it."

The earl made some remark which sounded remarkably like a grunt.

Freddie's enchantment fled, leaving her feeling small and unwanted. "Are we to go home?" she ventured miserably.

"We are invited to take a late supper with a Major and Mrs. Tulley. Of course, if you would rather return home, I can make your apologies."

"No, I shall be happy to go," said Freddie, sounding as miserable as anyone could be.

"I sent them word of our engagement," said the earl. "They are good friends of mine and would be surprised if they read the notice in the journals tomorrow before hearing anything about it from me."

"Our engagement in the newspapers?" said Freddie. "So soon?"

"I sent a servant with the announcement before I even went to the Oakleys'."

"Before?" Freddie looked at him in amazement. "You didn't even think to propose to me," she said, lowering her voice as several members of the audience began to look at her curiously. "You did not think I might refuse?"

"You have no alternative," he said coldly. "And neither have I. Shall we go?"

Miss Manson watched their angry faces in trepidation. If they continued like this, she thought, undoubtedly she would be forced to set off on another adventure with Freddie.

Would her married life be like this? thought Freddie gloomily. Being ordered here and there without her wishes ever being consulted.

The Tulleys came as a pleasant surprise. The major was thin and ascetic-looking and had little to say, but he had a restful manner and was a good listener. Mrs. Tulley was much younger than her husband, a good-natured brunette who teased the earl about having fallen in love at last.

The earl took her bantering in good part. He seemed more at ease than he had been for some time and entertained the company with a description of amusing plays he had seen.

"I gather you enjoyed Kean's *Hamlet*," said Major Tulley to Freddie after the earl had finished.

"Very much," she replied. "It was *electric*."

"Oh, don't talk of electricity." Mrs. Tulley laughed. "Or my husband will subject you to his latest toy. It's an electrifying machine."

"How does it work?" Freddie asked curiously. "So many people seem to believe that electricity cures everything from agues to blindness."

The major showed more animation than he had all evening. "I do not think it can do any of these things, but I do believe it helps the circulation of the blood. With your permission, Miss Armstrong, I will give you a little demonstration. It is quite harmless, you know."

Freddie nodded eagerly. The major rang the bell, and soon a manservant returned with a small machine that had a cranking handle. Freddie looked at it curiously. Electricity was still very much an amusement, although in some cases a dangerous one. She could remember her grandfather telling her about all the people who had been killed in the last century trying to emulate Benjamin Franklin by flying kites in thunderstorms. Some people even believed that an electric shock helped the growth of plants.

They were all seated in the Tulleys' comfortable drawing room. The machine was set in front of the fire.

"What do we do?" asked Miss Manson, looking nervously at the electrifying machine as if it might bite.

"Well, my wife will hold this wire while I crank the machine. You all form a chain, holding on to each other's hands. Let me see. Miss Manson, you hold my wife's hand, and Berham, you take Miss Manson's hand on one side and Miss Armstrong's on the other."

The major started cranking busily. Mrs. Tulley held on to the wire, rolling her eyes to heaven in mock resignation.

"Now," said the major.

The earl took Miss Manson's hand in his right and then half turned and held out his left hand to Freddie. She lowered her eyes and almost shyly put her hand into his, feeling his strong fingers closing about her own.

The earl felt a tingling sensation going up his

arm, and Freddie must have experienced the same sensation, for she looked up at him in surprise.

"What an odd machine!" exclaimed the earl. "The shock affects only my left side."

"Very odd," teased Mrs. Tulley, "for you see, I had dropped the wire by mistake. Ah, Lord Berham, what you are experiencing is the electricity of love."

"Nonsense!" said the earl. "It must have been a twinge of rheumatism."

"Of course," Freddie agreed sweetly. "At your great age such maladies are to be expected."

"Pay attention," called the major. To his wife, he said, "Please make sure you have the wire."

He began to crank the handle furiously. Everyone experienced a mild but unpleasant shock. Miss Manson screamed and fell forward on the floor, her skirt rucking up at the back, to reveal a pair of matchstick legs encased in green silk stockings.

And that's something else to lay at Clarissa Rennenord's door, thought the earl, looking down at Miss Manson with disfavor. *She* had recommended Miss Manson. If he dismissed Miss Manson, she would no doubt think the fickle aristocracy was being heartless again. Why did people never examine their own faults? thought the earl savagely. Why did they always blame other people for their misfortunes?

Take Miss Frederica Armstrong, for instance.

She should be grateful to him. Yes, grateful! Did she realize the full extent of the honor that had been conferred on her? He glanced down at her, surprised again to find himself looking at a beautiful young woman instead of the tomboyish schoolgirl he always seemed to think her.

Her gown was of pale straw-colored silk. It was cut across the bosom in such a way as to reveal the charms of high, firm little breasts.

He remembered how that ridiculous ball gown she had worn had revealed all her charms and found himself suddenly prey to what he could only damn as an intense fit of lust.

This would never do, he chided himself as the others, including a vastly recovered Miss Manson, crowded around the machine to examine it. He had been celibate too long. When they were married, he would see about setting up a mistress. But what if Freddie took a lover?

He looked at her again. She was bending over the machine, the silk of her gown tight across her bottom. He half closed his eyes. How old Colonel Armstrong would gloat!

It has all hit me at once, mused the earl. I have been thinking of her as a sort of boy for so long.

And yet he remembered her kneeling in front of him all those months ago at Berham Court and recalled how his feelings towards the "youth" at his feet had alerted him to the fact that she was a girl. He had to admit, she had held a certain attraction for him even then.

"I say, Berham," called the major. "Don't you

want to examine this? Feel any better for your shock?"

"No," said the earl, thinking only of the shock to his senses caused by Miss Frederica Armstrong. He went over and crouched down by the machine while the others stood back to give him a better view.

Freddie looked wistfully down at his thick black hair and the strong line of his profile, at his broad shoulders set off by the exquisite tailoring of his blue coat, at the strong thighs encased in tight pantaloons, at the strong, capable hands with the great crested ring on the middle finger of the right one as they examined the machine.

Grandfather was wrong, thought Freddie. Men were not the only ones consumed by lustful feelings.

Miss Manson covertly watched both of them. She had caught the earl looking at her in a disapproving way, and all her old fears had come rushing back. Lady Rennenord had not lost any time spreading malicious gossip. She probably had sent a letter to Berham asking Mrs. Bellisle to close the cottage.

Once again the future yawned like a great black pit at Miss Manson's feet.

Only look how Freddie studied the earl with that wistful, hungry look. Only see the way the earl did not look at Freddie, and yet every bit of his body seemed to be intensely aware of her presence. Unless something happened, this intense feeling each had for the other could drive them violently apart instead of into each other's arms.

Pride, thought Miss Manson, nodding her head wisely. That's all it is. Pride and wounded feelings.

The earl looked around at that moment and caught Miss Manson nodding wisely to herself.

The woman's quite mad, he thought, looking at her with dislike.

Miss Manson caught that look and became even more terrified. She must do something. But what?

It was a silent threesome who made their way back to Berkeley Square after saying good-bye to the Tulleys.

As soon as they had arrived, the earl muttered, "Good night." Without looking at either Miss Manson or Freddie, he strode off into the library and shut the door.

Freddie looked after him, her hands hanging at her sides, her mouth drooping in disappointment. Then she turned to Miss Manson.

"We will leave tomorrow," she said, half to herself. "I am so weary now, I think I shall go straight to sleep. It is not fair, Miss Manson. I am a prey to self-pity. All the villains of this piece seem to escape scot-free. Lady Rennenord has succeeded in her revenge. That awful captain and those terrible Hope sisters are free to prey on more unsuspecting people. . . . Oh, I shall be *glad* to get away."

Miss Manson watched her go, her brain working furiously. If only there were some way to force the earl and Frederica to be together even for a short while. Perhaps then the earl might realize how much he loved the girl.

Miss Manson looked at the clock and saw that it was three in the morning. A new day. Today was the day of the May Fair, the day on which all the servants were allowed to go. From eleven in the morning until five in the evening there would not be a servant in the house. And Freddie, like most of London society, often slept until noon.

Miss Manson started on a tour of inspection while she laid plans.

What she had in mind just might work.

Chapter 9

Captain Cramble sat up on the box of a hired carriage and thought gloomily about its occupants.

Ever since they had left London he had had a feeling of foreboding. Miss Mary had insisted on taking possession of the leather bag with the jewels. The captain felt somewhere in his fat soul that it was only a matter of time before the sisters would decide to give him the slip or, worse, kill him.

He longed for a drink, but the sisters had ordered him not to stop until three in the afternoon, when they should have left London and all its Bow Street Runners a safe way behind.

His mind turned this way and that. He was sure they would not harm him until he had arranged a passage for them all on a boat at Dover. He pulled his watch out of his waistcoat. Only half an hour to go. How could a man be expected to think with a sober head?

He had first met the sisters when he had called at the seminary, searching for clues to Freddie's where-abouts. He had come across them again by chance when all were hiding out in a thieves' kitchen on the moors above Lamstowe, and they had agreed to join forces.

They had decided not to try to sell the jewels in England. Once they were abroad, it would be easier to do so without attracting the attention of the law.

He toyed with the idea of hitting them over the head once they got to the inn and then escaping with the jewels, but Miss Mary held the purse strings. It would be wiser to allow her to pay all the expenses until they reached the coast. Then he would be shot of them.

But in case they tried any tricks on him first, he wanted to be sure of having the diamonds.

At last the posting house they had decided on, the Six Tuns, hove into view at a bend in the road.

The captain turned into the inn yard and set about arranging a fresh team while the sisters went into the inn to see about rooms. Once they were all settled in a private parlor and enjoying a hearty dinner, the captain suggested that they go to bed early and have a good night's rest so that they might make an early start at dawn.

"You'd better let me keep the jewels," he said. "If there are any villains about, they're more likely to attack two defenseless females."

Miss Mary hesitated, looking at him with cold, calculating eyes. "Very well," she said thoughtfully, "but to ensure *your* safety, Captain, I am sure you will not object to us locking you in your room."

"Not at all," said the captain cheerfully, an idea having just struck him. "I'll take a turn about the yard before I retire. I would like to blow a cloud, and I know you ladies can't stand the smell of smoke."

Once in the yard, the captain lit a cheroot and began to amble up and down, glancing occasionally up at the inn windows. From time to time he would bend down, pick up a handful of pebbles, and stuff them into one of his capacious pockets.

At last he went back upstairs to join them. Miss Mary handed him the leather bag, and then both sisters marched him to his room, inspected the window to make sure the captain could not possibly get his great bulk through it, and then left, taking the key and locking him in.

The captain sat by the window for a long time, making sure they had no intention of returning.

He opened the bag and took out the diamond tiara and the diamond collar. Then he took out a sharp knife and got to work. He prized every gem free of its setting and spread them around the many pockets of his coat. Then he returned the denuded settings to the bag and added the pebbles he had collected and piled on a table to the bag, hefting it in his hand until he was sure he had the correct weight. Then he opened the window and tossed the remaining stones out into the yard.

He was awakened at four in the morning by Miss Cassandra. They were setting out while it was still dark, she said.

Grumbling, the captain finally hoisted himself up on the box. Miss Mary had not looked in the bag. He sincerely hoped she would not think of doing so before they reached Dover.

It was still dark. A warm, gusty wind was blowing from the south, bringing with it the smell of flowers and leaves and approaching rain.

A great flash of lightning lit up the surrounding countryside as he turned out of the inn yard, followed by an earth-shaking crack of thunder.

Inside the coach, Miss Cassandra let out a faint scream.

Captain Cramble devoutly hoped both ladies were scared of storms. With good luck their fear would keep them too occupied to look at the contents of the leather bag.

A great blinding sheet of rain struck the horses and carriage. Lightning split the darkness again, and the horses reared and plunged.

The captain was debating whether to turn about and head for the shelter of the inn when another flash of lightning lit up the road ahead, showing two tall figures on horseback, barring his way.

Highwaymen!

The captain gave a gasp and clumsily began to try to turn the coach. But it was slewed across the road, unable to go backwards or forwards, when the two highwaymen rode up.

He slumped over the reins, trying to look as much like a hired coachman as possible.

He looked down into the masked face of one

of the men, shrugged, and jerked his thumb towards the carriage door as if to say, "There's where your money is." But one kept him covered with a pistol while the other wrenched open the door.

The Hope sisters stumbled out into the drenching rain.

The captain turned his head away. These men were hardened criminals. Occasionally impoverished gentlemen took to the road and prided themselves on having a certain gallantry when it came to dealing with the ladies, but these two were ruffians. Both the carriage and Miss Mary and Miss Cassandra were ruthlessly searched. All their money was taken, along with their trinkets and jewelry.

Then one of the highwaymen lifted out the bare settings and looked at them curiously. He tilted the bag and shook out a pile of pebbles onto his hand.

Another flash of lightning showed both sisters, the empty settings, and the pebbles.

"You stole them," screamed Miss Mary over the sound of the storm. "Thief!" She pointed up at the crouched figure of the captain on the box.

"Fool!" said Miss Cassandra bitterly. "You *fool*, Mary. If you'd kept your trap shut, we could've had them off him later."

But it was too late. The captain was already being ordered down from the box.

"Turn out your pockets, my brave cully," snarled the leader.

The captain looked at the highwayman's pistol, but it never wavered. Slowly he turned out each pocket, passing over pile after pile of gems.

When he got to the last pocketful, he took them out slowly and suddenly hurled them full in the highwayman's face. He turned and took off down the road as fast as his short little legs could carry him.

"Let him be," growled the other highwayman, picking up the jewels. "Loose the horses from the coach, Jemmy."

The one called Jemmy took out a knife, cut the traces, and yelled and shouted at the horses. Already frightened by the storm, the animals took off and galloped down the road, bunched together, in the direction of the inn.

Still keeping the sisters covered with their pistols, the highwaymen swung themselves up on their horses.

"They'll tell the law on us," said the one called Jemmy. "Shall I shoot 'em?"

"Naw," said his companion, looking at the shivering sisters with contempt. "Bunch o' thieves, that's wot they are. Tryin' to double-cross each other."

Both men swung about and rode off into the storm. Miss Mary and Miss Cassandra stood for quite a long time in the rain, each abusing the other.

The thunderstorm which had plagued the sisters and Captain Cramble rolled into London at six in the morning. Miss Manson lay tossing and turning. If it continued, the May Fair would be canceled. It was no longer the great fair it had been in former years.

At last, unable to bear the worry, she got up and dressed herself and went to sit by the window. It should have been light, it should have been dawn, but the black clouds seemed to lie on the tops of the very houses.

Miss Manson's bedroom was near the top of the tall house, so she had an excellent view across the rooftops of the West End of London.

When eight o'clock struck and she was weary with waiting and watching, a roof in the far distance suddenly turned to gold, then another, and another.

The clouds parted, and Miss Manson dreamily watched a little patch of blue sky grow bigger and bigger. The rain ceased as abruptly as it had started. The thunder gave a faint, disgruntled roar like some great beast retreating to its cave in the sky.

Golden water chuckled in the gutters. Across the square, a housemaid threw up a window and shook out a rug.

Miss Manson fell into a light sleep, waking with a start at the bustle and noise outside. She opened the window and looked out. The servants were crowding up the area steps, dressed in their finery. She counted them carefully, making sure no one had been left behind. At last they were all gone.

She took a deep breath and straightened her cap. She made her way to Frederica's bedroom, squared her shoulders, wrenched open the door, and rushed in.

"Oh, Frederica, my love," she cried. "Please awake. My lord is ill!"

Freddie woke immediately. "Where? What?"

"Come quickly," gasped Miss Manson. "Lord Berham . . . oh, it is too terrible."

She turned and ran from the room. Frightened out of her wits, Freddie ran after her.

Miss Manson ran along the passageway and threw open the door of Lord Berham's bedroom. Freddie rushed past her and into the room.

Miss Manson quietly closed the door firmly behind her and locked it. She pocketed the heavy key and, mumbling a silent prayer, went off to the head of the stairs. She would return in a few minutes to listen at the door and see whether her plan had worked.

Freddie was not aware of the door closing. She stood with her hand to her mouth, looking at Lord Berham's still face against the pillow. What if he were dead?

She glanced around and, not seeing Miss Manson, assumed that she had gone to get help.

"Augustus," she said in a trembling voice, using his Christian name for the first time. "I am so sorry I have been such a plague to you. Oh, don't die."

His eyes flew open, and he stared at Freddie in amazement.

"Don't try to rise," she said as he struggled up against the pillows. She took his shoulders and tried to push him down into the bed again.

"Are you drunk?" he snapped. "What is going on?"

"Miss Manson awoke me. She said you were deathly ill."

"That woman's crazy. I am not ill. Now, will you leave me alone and go away."

Freddie realized that she was still holding him by the shoulders and that his shoulders were naked. "I was only concerned about your health," she said in a voice which now trembled with rage. She swung about and stalked to the door.

"It's locked," she said in a puzzled voice.

"You have more hair than wit," said the earl nastily. "Oh, turn your back while I get out of bed. *Women!*"

He slid into a long silk dressing gown and tied it firmly about his waist. "Now," he said, edging Freddie aside. He turned the handle and then wrenched it. It refused to budge.

He marched over to the fireplace and rang the bell. After a few moments had passed and no one came, the earl let out an oath. "The servants are all at the fair. Where's that Manson woman?" He kicked at the door with his bare foot, stubbed his toe, and hopped back across the room, swearing fluently.

Freddie giggled. "You do look funny."

"Well, unless that Manson woman comes to let us out, we are trapped in here until five

211

o'clock, and I hope *that* amuses you. Since there is nothing else to do, I am going back to sleep. *You* may do as you please."

Freddie looked at him mutinously and then walked to the window and pulled aside the curtains.

"Come away from there!" he said sharply. "That nightgown you are wearing is nigh transparent in the sunlight."

Freddie made a move to cover her breasts, and then her hands dropped to her sides. "What if it is?" she said defiantly. "The sight of my body is not going to rouse you to mad passion."

"Perhaps not," he said, "but do remember the passions of the watchman and stand away from the window."

"He can't see me from the street, and if he could, he might at least try to get in and help us."

"Are you not ashamed to be seen by me in such a state of undress?" asked the earl caustically.

Freddie was, but she was not going to let him know it. She looked him up and down. It was obvious he was wearing nothing under his robe.

"You don't seem to have much shame yourself," she said, emboldened by hurt and pique that they should be alone in his bedroom and that it should mean nothing to him.

"It's different for a man," he said crossly.

Freddie flounced over to a chair by the fire and sat down. The firelight flickered on the soft stuff of her gown, revealing tantalizing glimpses of her body. She leaned forward to put a lump of coal on the fire.

"Leave it," said the earl harshly. "This room is warm enough."

Indeed, he did look very warm. His face was flushed, and faint beads of perspiration stood out on his brow.

Freddie's anger fled, and she looked at him with quick concern. "Perhaps Miss Manson is right and you *are* ill." She walked over to him and stood on tiptoe and felt his brow.

The earl let out a groan.

"Oh, Augustus," said Freddie, throwing her arms about him. "I am a wicked girl. You are ill. You were merely being brave. I am going to open the window and scream for help. I am —"

He put his hands at her waist and held her a little away from him. She could feel the heat from his body and see the feverish flames flickering in his eyes.

"I am burning with desire," he said in a low voice. "Oh, Frederica, you do not know how utterly seductive, adorable, and lovable you look at this moment."

He swept her into his arms and bent his mouth to hers.

For at least half an hour the tremendous passion which consumed them both was a little assuaged by kissing and kissing as if they would never stop. Lips burned against lips, body fused against body, arms clutched, and hands explored.

Miss Manson crouched outside the door with her ear to the keyhole.

"I love you, Freddie," said the earl, freeing his mouth.

Miss Manson gave a little sigh of relief and unlocked the door. The earl heard the key click in the lock but made no move to release his hold on Freddie.

"When did you know you loved me?" asked Freddie.

"Only just now, but I think I must have loved you the first time I saw you and did not know it. Do you mind my calling you Freddie? It's an odd name for a girl, but I always think of you as Freddie; willful, adorable, and very dear."

"Kiss me again," murmured Freddie. "And you can call me anything you please. I love you so much."

"I am afraid of frightening you," he said gently. "I am afraid your grandfather has given you a disgust of . . . certain intimacies."

"Like this," whispered Freddie, sliding her hand inside his dressing gown and caressing his chest.

Another hectic half hour passed until the earl, looking tenderly down at her, traced the line of her bruised and swollen lips with his fingertip.

"No," he said softly as Freddie looked hopefully towards the bed.

"No?"

"No," he repeated firmly, trapping one of her

wandering hands. "We can wait until our wedding night. We will be married very soon and not in any haveycavey manner but with the whole of London to see us."

"Oh, Augustus, since we are to be married in any case —"

"No, my wanton. And since the crafty Miss Manson unlocked the door some time ago, having achieved what she set out to achieve, I think we should get dressed and go out and enjoy the sunshine."

"Clever Miss Manson," murmured Freddie. "This is the second time she has come to my rescue."

"Oh, I would have come to my senses sooner or later."

"But perhaps *too* late." Freddie grinned. "I was going to run away."

"I would have found you, and punished you."

"Punished me? You would beat me?"

"I would kiss you, quite fiercely, here . . . and here . . . and here."

Miss Manson paced up and down the hall below, clutching and unclutching her hands. Any minute now the earl would descend with the awful news of her dismissal. She now felt sure he would never forgive such impertinence.

But at least she had a clear conscience. She had done something courageous. She had helped Freddie as much as she could, even though she had realized at the last moment that the outcome might mean happiness for Freddie but would certainly mean the end of her job as Freddie's companion.

Miss Manson glanced at the clock and wrung her hands. It was now nearing five. Soon the servants would be home, and she did not want them to be witness to the terrible row that the earl was sure to give her.

Then she heard steps on the landing above. This was it. She bent her head submissively and waited for the axe to fall.

"My dear Miss Manson," came the earl's light, amused voice. "We are going out driving, and how can you possibly come with us and chaperone my ward while you do not even have a bonnet on?"

Miss Manson looked up. The earl and Freddie were standing with their arms linked, dressed to go out. Freddie's face was blazing with love and happiness, and the earl raised her hand to his lips and kissed it.

"Well, Miss Manson," he said gently. "We are waiting."

"Oh, yes," gabbled Miss Manson gratefully. "Very good, my lord. Certainly, my lord. I will be with you directly. I will fetch my bonnet and cloak and . . ."

She ran headlong for the stairs, tripping and stumbling in her haste.

"Poor woman," said Freddie. "You must not be angry with her."

"Nobody could make me angry today. I love the whole world."

Freddie stood on tiptoe to plant a kiss on the end of his nose. "No, you don't," she said. "You love only me, and I won't allow another woman within a yard of you, except Miss Manson."

"Who knows? I may develop a mad passion for Miss Manson."

"Oh, Augustus, kiss me again."

Miss Manson stood on the landing, clutching her gloves and turning pink with a mixture of pleasure and embarrassment. Then she coughed loudly and went down the stairs. Miss Manson was going to have to perfect that fake cough. It would be needed many times in the days to come.

And so they were married, one month later, with great pomp and circumstance in St. George's Hanover Square.

They returned to the townhouse in Berkeley Square, and Freddie soon had her final lesson in the facts of life, the start of a long and pleasurable schooling.

As she lay warm and content in his arms after a tumultuous night, hearing the sparrows squabbling in the gutters and the hoarse cry of the watch, Freddie murmured languidly, "It has all turned out so beautifully. I wish everyone in the world were as happy as I, except Lady Rennenord and those two Hope sisters, and let us not forget Captain Cramble."

"They'll get their comeuppance," said the earl sleepily. "Villains don't escape forever." She stirred against him, and he looked down at her with a wicked gleam in his eyes. "What's this, my sweeting? Wouldst die of passion?"

"Why not?" demanded the countess of Berham.

"Why not, indeed?" said the earl of Berham, sliding her nightgown down over her shoulders.

Captain Cramble was already dead. He had contracted an inflammation of the lungs after being drenched in the storm. The two Hope sisters had set sail for America after a weary journey on foot to Dover. Penniless and destitute, they had arrived at Dover, where a very kind gentleman had taken them under his wing. He knew the captain of a vessel bound for the New World, he had said. The good captain would give them free passage, and he would arrange for them to be met at the other side.

Cassandra and Mary gladly agreed. By the time they realized they were being sold as slaves, it was too late. Mary did not survive the long passage. The conditions aboard the ship were appalling, for white-slaves only fetched fourteen pounds sterling. Since one could sell a good black for one hundred and forty-four pounds, no one was particularly anxious about the welfare of the whites.

Cassandra became servant to a woman in Connecticut who was louder, more tyrannical, and more bullying than she herself had ever been.

The earl bought the cottage from Mrs. Bellisle

and presented it to Miss Manson in the hope that she would retire to it as soon as possible.

Lady Rennenord eventually married a rich merchant, not finding out until the knot was well and truly tied that he was an incredible miser. She did not even have a visit from her brother to look forward to, since she had told Harry Struthers-Benton never to call again. For on his last visit, all he had done was prattle on insensitively and endlessly about what a deuced happy couple Lord and Lady Berham were, and about how their love match was the talk of the town.